Sasha doesn't want a mate. He barely even wants friends, but he's given up on trying to keep them out of his life. He's content as he is, working at the bar in Gillham and going home to his empty apartment. It's better that way, and safer—for everyone. Because Sasha has a secret, and he's already responsible for one death, and he doesn't want anything like that to happen again.

Hunter has always been content with hookups and one-night stands. He's never really thought about finding his mate—until he does. Sasha is standoffish, and while Hunter wishes he were an easier man to deal with, he's ready to wait as long as he needs to in order to have him in his life. Still, when he and his team are sent on a mission in the Brazilian rainforest, he hopes that will give Sasha enough time to make a decision about them.

Sasha realizes he's made a mistake by pushing Hunter away when Hunter doesn't come back from the mission. Hunter is stuck in a rainforest crawling with members of the Beasts gang, and he needs help. Will Sasha be able to help him, or will he lose Hunter before he even has him?

The unauthorized reproduction or distribution of this copyrighted work is illegal. Criminal copyright infringement, including infringement without monetary gain, is investigated by the FBI and is punishable by up to 5 years in federal prison and a fine of $250,000.

This book is a work of fiction. Names, characters, places, and incidents either are products of the author's imagination or are used fictitiously. Any resemblance to actual events or locales or persons, living or dead, is entirely coincidental.

Sasha
Copyright © 2019 Catherine Lievens
ISBN: 978-1-4874-2409-1
Cover art by Angela Waters

All rights reserved. Except for use in any review, the reproduction or utilization of this work in whole or in part in any form by any electronic, mechanical or other means, now known or hereafter invented, is forbidden without the written permission of the publisher.

Published by eXtasy Books Inc or
Devine Destinies, an imprint of eXtasy Books Inc

Look for us online at:
www.eXtasybooks.com or www.devinedestinies.com

Sasha
Council Enforcers Book 18

By

Catherine Lievens

Chapter One

Sasha slid the beer over the counter and nodded at the woman. She grinned at him and leaned closer, exposing more of her cleavage. "Thank you."

He smiled at her and turned. She was cute, but so not his type. She didn't have a dick.

"Hey man."

Sasha turned toward the next customer, his smile widening when he saw Grey. "Hey." Sasha touched his hair, making sure it was still in place, and he got closer. "What can I do for you?"

Grey waved toward a spot behind him. "There's a group of us tonight."

"How many beers?"

Grey chucked. "You know us so well."

"It's my job."

"I don't know. I thought I was more than a job for you." He pressed his hand to his chest. "You wound me, Sasha."

Sasha rolled his eyes. "Are you going to order? Because as you can see, the place is packed, and I have other customers." Sasha wouldn't have dared to speak like that to customers, but Grey wasn't only that. Sasha considered him a friend, kind of, and he knew that went for Grey, too. They didn't hang out much, but that was more because Sasha tended to isolate himself, even from friends.

Grey gave Sasha his order. Sasha wished he could go over to the table Grey shared with his friends and sit with them, but it was Friday night, and he wouldn't be able to take his break for a while. Still, he couldn't look away as Grey grabbed the beer bottles and left with a nod. He was there with his mate and a few other people, and Sasha's gaze went straight to Hunter.

He knew he shouldn't be staring. He knew he shouldn't even be *thinking* about Hunter. There was no way Hunter would ever want to take him back to the bathroom like he did so often with other guys, and Sasha didn't want that. No, Sasha had given up on love. He didn't deserve it. But damn if he didn't miss it.

He shook his head. The only reason he missed having love in his life was because he hadn't been strong enough, and he wasn't going to make that mistake again. Besides, even if he wanted to, Hunter had never given him a second glance, and that was okay.

Hunter might be Sasha's type—or rather, he was *anyone's* type, with that long, blond hair and those mischievous eyes—but Sasha had never been into playboys. Hunter had a different guy with him every time he came to the bar, and when he didn't have one, he found one on the premises. Sasha had always hated being a notch on a belt, even when he'd been a college kid.

That hadn't changed.

"How are things going?" Nate asked, slipping behind the bar.

Sasha pressed his lips together. He wasn't going to smile. "You're late."

"That's one of the perks of being the boss."

"I should ask for a raise. You've abandoned me to the crowd without a second thought."

Nate laughed and punched Sasha's shoulder. "Shut up. You're more than able to wrangle them."

"Doesn't mean I wouldn't rather have help."

Nate patted Sasha's shoulder. "You have it now, so stop

complaining and get back to work."

Sasha did. It was easy to lose himself in the steady rhythm of taking orders, handing out drinks, and taking money. This was his job. He did it almost every night, and he didn't have to focus on it anymore.

"Hey, pretty," a man drawled.

Sasha suppressed a sigh. "What can I get you?"

"How about your phone number?"

Sasha almost rolled his eyes, but he didn't want Nate to lose a customer because he couldn't keep his reactions to himself. "I meant to drink."

"Whatever you'll have."

"I'm working. I can't drink."

"I'm sure you can take a break and sit with me."

"I'm sorry."

Sasha turned to tell Nate to take the guys' order, but the man reached out, catching Sasha's long hair and pulling on it none too gently. "Come on, pretty boy. Show me what you're hiding under that hair, yeah?"

Sasha jerked back, and thankfully, the man let go of his hair. He'd seen, though. Sasha could tell by the horror on his face. He was ready to bet the asshole wasn't so eager to have a drink with him now.

"What the fuck is going on here?" Nate's voice boomed.

The man raised his hands. "Nothing. I was just ordering a drink."

"Sasha?"

From the look Nate gave him, he could tell there was more than that happening, but Sasha wasn't going to say anything. "I'm okay."

"You sure?"

"Yeah."

"Why don't you take your break now?"

Sasha risked a glance at the guy who'd touched him, and

sure enough, he was looking everywhere but at him. He'd changed his mind as soon as he'd seen the scar.

Sasha didn't blame him. He knew it was ugly. He was mostly used to it by now, but sometimes, especially first thing in the morning, it still made him jolt when he saw himself in the mirror. "I can work."

Nate glared at the man who was now ignoring them. "Take your break. It's only fair, since you had to deal with the crowd on your own until now."

Sasha wasn't going to refuse twice. He didn't think it was necessary, but it was a relief, even though he was used to people's reactions when they first saw his scar. Some pitied him, some were disgusted. Most didn't know where to look or how to behave, as if the scar changed who he was as a person, as if it made him not quite human.

He nodded. "Okay. Thanks."

"Take your time. Have something to eat. The crowd isn't going anywhere."

Sasha took his apron off and left the area behind the bar. He looked straight ahead, just in case the man who'd touched him was looking at him, but he doubted he would. He wasn't as pretty as he'd seemed to be, and that was what that man had been after—a pretty face.

The hallway leading to the break room was quieter than the bar, but not by much. Sasha looked down, his hair sliding in front of him and hiding his scar, just in case someone came out of the bathroom while he was there. He managed to slip into the break room without encountering anyone, though.

He closed the door and leaned back against it, taking a deep breath and closing his eyes.

He was okay. He was always okay. The scar was just that—a scar. He didn't care about it, except because of the way it made people look at him—and for what it reminded him of. He still had nightmares about that day, and he always would. He couldn't forget, not when the reminder was so obvious on his face—and when he'd lost some of his vision because of the wound that had caused the scar.

He swallowed and opened his eyes. He saw well enough, even with his compromised eye. He could work and live normally—something he'd always felt he didn't deserve.

He shook his head. He had to stop doing this. He couldn't think about Cedric right now, not if he wanted to be able to finish his shift. He *needed* to finish it, because he needed the tips to pay rent and buy food. He'd have the time to cry once he was home, alone in his bed.

But first, food.

Sasha opened his locker and got out the sandwich he'd brought from home. He knew he could go to the kitchen and ask Lydia to whip something up for him, but she was busy with the customers, and he didn't want to take her away from that. He could get some fries when the evening started winding down and people left the bar. He was in no hurry to go back to the crowd out there, and he hoped Nate wouldn't mind it if he spent a bit more time in the break room.

Sometimes, quiet time was all that got him through the night.

Hunter didn't look back when he left the bathroom. He'd made sure the guy who'd sucked him off was okay—and that he'd come, too—but that was it. He didn't know the guy and would probably ever see him again.

He grinned at Grey and Patrick, who were hanging around waiting for him. He punched Patrick on the shoulder. The man had surprised him in a good way. He hadn't been sure this was a good idea when he'd left the stall door slightly open for Grey like he always did when they spent the evening together and he brought someone to the bathroom, and he'd been stunned to see not only Grey watching him but also Patrick. He'd half-expected Patrick to freak out at some point, start spouting insults and maybe let his fists fly. It wouldn't have been the first time. Grey had a way of picking the worst men when it came to his kink, so much that Hunter knew he'd started thinking he wasn't right in the head because of it.

What a crock of bullshit. As far as Hunter was concerned, what happened in someone's bedroom—or a bar's bathroom in this case—was their business, and their business only. As long as everyone agreed and was legal, everything was possible.

He hadn't expected Patrick, a detective in their small town, to agree with him on that. "Enjoyed that, did you?" he teased. "And don't tell me you're one of those guys who doesn't want to talk about it because it's embarrassing." Hunter wouldn't have been surprised.

"I'm not. I don't want to talk about it because my sex life is only my business and Grey's. You were just some nice porn, as far as I'm concerned."

Hunter laughed. Damn, he liked Patrick. The guy would be great for Grey. He wouldn't judge him, and from the looks of it, he'd even be an eager participant. "Damn right. I guess you're leaving?" He'd noticed the way Grey and Patrick were behaving, and he knew they'd want to be alone to fuck each other's brains out. He wished he could see that, but he doubted Patrick would want that. Besides, it wasn't what Grey wanted, either. He liked to watch, not to be watched.

"We are," Patrick confirmed.

Hunter pouted a bit, but he was happy for Grey. He was one of his best friends, and not only because of the kink thing. He liked Grey, and he knew he wouldn't be able to spend as much time with him as he had before. Grey had found his mate, and his world centered around Patrick, now — as was right. Patrick's life was all about Grey, and Grey deserved it.

Still, Hunter couldn't help but tease as they headed back toward the bar. "Can I come to watch?"

Patrick narrowed his eyes. "I'm not going to ask what."

"Because you already know. Come on. It would be hot."

"Possibly. Doesn't mean I want anyone else seeing Grey naked. Not even you. No offense."

"None taken."

A door opened just before they passed by it and the barman stepped out, almost slamming against Hunter's chest.

Hunter had noticed him before — how could he not have? Sasha was gorgeous, and he hadn't looked twice at Hunter, something that didn't happen often. That was the reason Hunter had left him alone. He clearly wasn't interested in a quick bathroom hook-up. It was a pity, but Hunter could understand that.

Hunter reached out to steady Sasha even though he didn't seem to need it. Then he froze.

He'd never been close enough to Sasha to smell him. Grey was usually the one who went up to the bar to grab drinks, because he and Sasha were friends and it gave him an opportunity to chat for a bit.

But now Hunter *was* close enough, and Sasha smelled of rain and sadness, of something warm that made Hunter want to wrap him in blankets and keep in his bed.

He smelled of Hunter's mate. He *was* Hunter's mate.

Sasha smiled at Grey, but then he looked at Hunter. Hunter tried to make his mouth work, but he couldn't. The only thing he seemed to be able to do right then was stare, and he knew it made him look like a creep.

"You were on break?" Grey said, breaking the silence.

Sasha looked away from Hunter, and Hunter wanted to beg him to turn back around. He wanted to see more of his mate. He wanted—he didn't know what he wanted. His mind was a mess, and Sasha's closeness wasn't helping.

"Yes, but I have to get back to work before Nate gets swamped."

"I'll give you a call later if I don't catch you before I leave, then."

Sasha smiled. "Sure."

He turned to leave, but Hunter didn't want him to. He wanted him to come back, and he wanted to talk to him. He moved to go after him, but the bathroom door opened, and the guy Hunter had been with came out. He smiled like the cat who got the cream when he saw Hunter there and sauntered toward him. "Hey, gorgeous. I didn't think you'd still be here."

Hunter groaned. He should have run before the guy came out, dammit. He'd known this was going to go this way. "I was just leaving."

"Why don't you give me your number before you go? I'm sure we can have a repeat."

"Not into repeats, sorry." Hunter turned and left as fast as he could, ignoring Patrick's snickers and the guy still calling after him.

He'd hoped to be able to talk to Sasha now that he'd gotten rid of the other guy, but Sasha was already back behind the bar serving drinks. Hunter huffed and stared at him, wondering if he could interrupt him. He wanted to, but Sasha was working. Hunter would have hated being interrupted at work.

"What's going on?" Grey asked, taking Hunter's arm and dragging him back to their table.

Hunter let him and flopped into the chair he'd left earlier. He raked a hand through his hair and pushed it away from his face, pulling on the strands. He couldn't look away from Sasha. He didn't *want* to look away.

Grey rapped his knuckles on the table. "Hunter. Focus. What's going on?"

"What do you think is going on, Grey? He's my mate."

Patrick made a strangled noise. "We just watched you have sex with your mate?" He looked horrified.

It took Hunter a second to realize what Patrick was saying. Then he laughed. "God, no. I meant Sasha."

Patrick's eyes widened and his gaze slid to the bar.

Hunter sighed happily and stared some more. He wanted to talk with his mate, but he could limit himself to watching him. He didn't mind, and he probably *should* take a moment to think.

He'd never thought about his mate. He was relatively young for a shifter, just forty-one, and he had a long life in front of him—that was, if nothing happened to him while he was on the job. Being an enforcer could be dangerous. But even without considering his job, Hunter had never really thought about settling down. He'd never met a man he'd want to settle with. He'd never considered the possibility.

Yet, here he was now, watching his mate and wondering what the fuck he was going to do.

"Hunter?" Grey's voice was gentle, as if he didn't want to startle Hunter.

Hunter turned to look at him. "Yes?"

"Are you okay?"

"I'm not sure."

Grey squeezed one of Hunter's hands. "Don't rush into anything now. Finding your mate is a shock, I know. You should give yourself a little time to think."

"Is that what you did?"

Grey and Patrick looked at each other. "No, it's not what I did. I told Patrick he was my mate almost as soon as I realized it."

"Then why shouldn't I?"

Grey hesitated. "Sasha isn't Patrick."

"I know that."

"There's something in his past. You saw his scar."

"I don't care about that." Hunter really didn't. It didn't take away from Sasha's beauty. Besides, Hunter would have wanted Sasha even if he'd looked like a monster. He'd never cared about what someone looked like, and he still didn't.

"I know you don't. What I was trying to say is that something happened to Sasha, and even I don't know what it is. But he got hurt, and I suspect he won't appreciate you barreling into his life like a bull in a china shop. Take the evening to calm down and think about what you want. You know where to find him. He's not going anywhere, but you might scare him off if you go in too strong."

Hunter wanted to disregard Grey's words, but Grey knew Sasha better than he did, so he nodded.

Sasha couldn't help sneaking glances toward the table where Hunter was seated. He didn't know why, but it had to do with what had happened in the hallway.

He wasn't sure what that was, though.

Nothing had been strange. Sasha said hello to Grey, and he'd smiled at Hunter. He didn't think he'd ever been so close to him. He wasn't sure that mattered. But there was something about Hunter, something Sasha had never realized, and now that he'd been close to him, he didn't seem to be able to stop thinking about him.

It was a bad idea. Sasha shouldn't be thinking about Hunter. It wouldn't bring him anything good.

For one, he wasn't looking for a boyfriend, or even for a one-night stand. And second, even if he were, he wouldn't go to Hunter. Hunter had a new man in his bed or in the bathroom every time he was there. Sasha didn't think he'd ever seen him with the same guy twice, or even for more than half an hour. But even if Sasha could get over that, why would Hunter look at him twice?

The man could have the most beautiful guys. Hell, he'd probably already had them. Sasha was far from being beautiful. He'd been cute enough before, but since the ... accident, the scars disfigured him. He was surprised Hunter had looked at him in the hallway, although maybe that was because he'd seen the scar on Sasha's face for the first time. Sasha tried to keep it hidden, after all.

Yes, that had to be it. Hunter had never seen the scar, and when he had, he'd been shocked, which was why he'd been staring. That was all that had happened.

Sasha wished he truly believed that. He couldn't help but notice that Hunter was still staring, though, or that he was having a hushed conversation with Grey, who was also looking his way.

What was happening? Was Grey trying to convince Hunter to leave Sasha alone? Sasha could see him doing something like that. He was a good friend, and he wouldn't want Sasha to get hurt. He knew Sasha wasn't looking for sex, so maybe he was warning Hunter away.

"Are you still thinking about the asshole from before?" Nate asked as he bumped his hip against Sasha's.

Sasha blinked and realized that instead of cleaning the counter like he'd meant to, he'd been staring into the distance—in the direction of Hunter's table. "Nope."

"Are you sure? Because you don't look too good. Are you coming down with something?"

"I feel fine. And I'm not going home, so don't even think about suggesting that." Nate could be overprotective sometimes. Sasha appreciated it—he didn't have anyone else in his life who cared as much as he did. They worked together and were nothing but boss and employee, although Sasha supposed that wasn't true anymore. Nate cared, just like he did.

Nate laughed and raised his hands. "All right, I won't say it. But you know you can go anytime if you're not feeling well."

"I know." Sasha was tempted. He wanted to escape Hunter's heavy gaze, but he couldn't leave Nate on his own to face the Friday night crowd. This was his job, and he was going to do it, no matter how he felt about it and everything else. He just needed to focus.

"Hey, Sasha."

Sasha looked up and smiled at Colin. "What are you doing here? You're not the bar type."

Colin's cheeks flushed, and he waved toward his mate, who stood beside him. "Matt wanted some time away from home. Jason's in a snit, and he won't talk to anyone. He just keeps slamming doors and listening to loud music, and Matt isn't used to being a stepfather yet."

Matt grimaced. "Don't put my name and the word father in the same sentence. I like your kids, but I'm *not* their dad."

Sasha smiled. It sounded like a well-oiled argument, as if Colin and Matt had discussed this time and time again. They probably had. They made Sasha think about how he and Cedric had been.

He shoved those memories away. There could be no thinking about Cedric, especially not while he was at work. He didn't need to be distracted that way. He couldn't start crying in front of everyone in the bar.

Colin frowned. "Are you okay?"

"Of course. What can I get you, then?"

"Something strong," Matt muttered.

Colin ignored him. "Are you sure? You looked . . . I don't

know. Lost, for a moment."

"Just tired. What are you drinking, then?"

"Two beers," Matt said.

Sasha was glad to see them sit at a table once they got their beers. He could feel Colin's worried gaze on him, but he ignored it.

There was nothing to worry about. He was just being overly dramatic about nothing important. Hunter would leave soon, and he wouldn't look back, just like he never had. He'd be back, and everything would be normal again. It had to be.

Sasha couldn't let himself think otherwise.

He tried to lose himself in his work, but it wasn't easy. He felt hyper-aware of Hunter's presence and what he was doing. He knew exactly when Hunter decided to leave because he was looking at him—again. He looked down when Hunter got up, not wanting to get caught watching him, but he couldn't resist peering up again.

Their gazes caught and held. Sasha couldn't look away. It was like Hunter's eyes were magnetic. He didn't think he could have looked away even if he'd wanted to, and he didn't. He wanted this last contact before Hunter left.

Grey pushed Hunter, and the contact was broken. Sasha swallowed and smiled at a customer, and the next time he looked up, Hunter was gone.

It was just as well. Sasha shouldn't be watching Hunter, and he shouldn't want him to come back.

The bar started emptying, and he was glad to see the customers leave. He was tired, more than usual. He couldn't believe it had to do with Hunter, though, so he chalked it up to the man who'd touched his hair. People didn't usually touch him like that. The guy had been rude and disrespectful, and Sasha needed to forget about him. He probably would never see him again anyway.

"Damn, I'm glad it's almost over," Nate said. He rubbed the back of his neck and tilted his head from side to side.

"You look tired."

"Not any more than you. I swear, sometimes I think I'm getting too old for this."

Sasha snorted. "Too old? You can't be more than thirty-something."

"Thirty-*something*?" Nate sounded amused.

Sasha waved his words away. "Late thirties?"

"More like early forties, but thanks for the confidence boost."

Sasha grinned. "You don't look that old."

Nate gaped, and Sasha moved away, still snickering. He was happy to be able to think about something that wasn't Hunter. Except there he was again, thinking about him. *Dammit.*

"You little shit," Nate muttered.

"Oh, come on. You love me."

Nate bumped their shoulders together. "You're right, I do."

"Don't make things awkward now."

Nate shook his head. "Not that way. You remind me of my little brother."

Nate never talked about his family, and Sasha wanted to know more. "Oh?"

Nate shrugged. "Mostly because he was younger. Let's start cleaning, yeah? The sooner we're done here, the sooner we can go home. I don't know about you, but I can't wait to get to bed."

Sasha's back and feet hurt. He wasn't in his early forties like Nate, but that didn't mean this job didn't take its toll on him. He *was* close to his thirties, after all. Sometimes he felt like he was eighty, though. Grief would do that to a man.

There were still a few lingering customers, just like every evening. It was still early, but Nate liked to close the bar around midnight. Gillham wasn't big, and the people who wanted to stay out later went to the clubs in the nearby towns. That was one of the reasons Sasha liked to work for him. He was home late, but not as late as he might have if he'd lived and worked in the city.

He was glad he'd moved to Gillham when he'd decided he couldn't stay in the apartment he'd shared with Cedric. It had hurt, because there'd been so many memories there, but he'd done the right thing.

His thoughts drifted back to Hunter, and he berated himself.

Or at least he hoped he'd done the right thing. Only the future would tell, though.

It was hard for him to leave the bar. Hunter would have never thought he'd feel this way, but he did. Well, he'd never thought about his mate, so he supposed it was normal. He wasn't sure he liked the longing to go back and wrap himself around Sasha and never let him go. He certainly felt like a creep over the thought, though.

"You're sure you don't want to sleep over?" Grey asked as they headed for Patrick's car.

He looked worried, so Hunter made sure to smile at him. "I'll be okay. Like you said, I need to think, so it's better if I do so in my bed."

Grey rolled his eyes. "You're going to fall asleep as soon as your head touches the pillow, but okay. Text me when you get there, though."

"Yes, Mom."

Grey tried to slap Hunter on the back of the head, but he ducked and stuck his tongue out at him.

He'd texted the mansion before leaving the bar, so all the Nix there would get the message, and one of them would come get him. He always felt a bit guilty at having them coming out to get him this late at night, but Dominic Nash, the Whitedell alpha, and Bran, the local head of the enforcers, wanted to make sure all the enforcers and pride members made it home okay, so it was a rule. Unless Hunter told them he was staying in Gillham, he had to send that text. He certainly didn't miss the two hours' drive to and from Gillham.

Grey and Patrick stayed with him until the Nix got there. Hunter grinned when Nysys appeared in front of him. He was wearing pink pajama pants with rainbows on them, a black t-shirt with a unicorn on the front, and bunny slippers. "You look ready for bed."

Nysys narrowed his eyes at him. "I am."

"Why are you here, then?"

"I wanted to see your flavor of the evening." He peered around Hunter. "Well? Where is he?"

"Still inside," Grey said before Hunter could tell Nysys to fuck off.

Hunter glared at him. "I didn't have a flavor of the night."

"Yes, you did. I was talking about the first guy."

Nysys' eyes sparkled. "The *first*? Oh, tell me all about this, please."

Hunter grabbed Nysys' hand. "Let's go. I'm tired."

Nysys pouted. "You're no fun." He looked at Grey and mouthed, "Call me."

Hunter elbowed him in the ribs. Nysys glared, but thank God, he waved at Grey and Patrick and finally shimmered them away.

Hunter let go of his hand as soon as they were home, but he should have known better than to think that Nysys would let him go without pushing. "Two, Hunter?" he teased.

Hunter sighed and rubbed his face. "One."

"What was Grey talking about, then?"

"Are you going to let it go if I don't tell you?"

"You know me better than that."

Hunter sighed. He did. Everyone knew Nysys. Once he dug his claws into something—a person, a bit of gossip—he didn't let go until he was satisfied. "I met someone."

Nysys' eyes widened. "You? The man who doesn't stick his dick in the same hole more than once?"

Hunter grimaced. "That makes it sound terrible."

"Because it is."

"Not everyone is happily mated like you." But Hunter might be soon, and he wasn't sure how he felt about that.

He didn't care about sex. He'd liked variety until now, but he didn't need it. It had just been easier. No one expected anything more than he gave, and he wanted it that way.

But Sasha would be different. He already was—and that thought terrified Hunter. He wasn't used to responsibilities, not when it came to his sex life. He'd never had anyone rely on him. Sasha was going to want to build a future together. He'd want a house, maybe even a family.

What the fuck was Hunter supposed to do with children?

"You look like you've seen a ghost," Nysys said. He leaned closer until his nose almost touched Hunter's. "Was it that bad? I assumed that the fact that you met someone would make you happy."

"Why should it?"

Nysys blinked and moved back. "Why not?"

"I don't know how this works, Nysys. I've never had a relationship. Even when I was younger, the longest I've been with someone is a few weeks. I have no idea what to do, how it works."

"Mmm. Okay. What do *you* want from this guy?"

"I don't know."

"Why is he different from the other people you've been with? I mean, he has to be if you've taken notice of him when you don't of the other people."

What would happen if Hunter told Nysys about Sasha? He'd be happy, but he'd probably also start shrieking as if someone was killing him, and people would come. He'd also never been able to keep his mouth shut, and the news would no doubt make the rounds of the mansion and the enforcers' wing. That was the last thing Hunter wanted. He didn't even know how he felt about it. He didn't want people to start congratulating him and all that stuff. He didn't want people to know, not yet.

"I'm tired," he said, pushing past Nysys.

Nysys huffed. "I'll find out anyway, you know."

"I have no doubt."

Hunter was glad to be away from Nysys. He liked the guy, but he was always sticking his nose in everyone's business. He did it because he wanted people to be happy, but that didn't mean it was enjoyable.

He should have known Nysys wasn't done with him.

He snuck into the enforcers' wing and went straight to his room. The place wasn't completely silent yet, and he could hear people talking, music, and the sound of TVs as he walked past the doors.

Michael was waiting for him when he got to his bedroom. He was sitting crossed-legged on Hunter's bed, his phone in his hand. He looked up when Hunter came in. "Hey. Nysys told me you needed me?"

Hunter rolled his eyes. "I hate that man."

"No, you don't. No one does. What's wrong?"

Hunter pushed his hair back. Michael was a member of his team, and the one he was closest to. He considered him one of his best friends, along with Grey, and Grey knew. The only reason Michael didn't was that he hadn't wanted to come to the bar tonight. "Nothing's wrong, exactly."

"But something did happen. Nysys doesn't usually worry for nothing."

Hunter flopped onto his bed next to Michael and took his boots off. "Yeah, okay, something happened."

"Are you going to tell me about it?"

"I don't want to. But yeah. I will. You have to promise you won't start jumping around, though. I'm . . . conflicted about it."

"I'll keep my mouth shut."

Hunter knew he would. Michael wasn't like Nysys. No one was, and thank God for that. "I met my mate tonight. You remember the guy who works at the bar, the one with the long hair?"

"The one with the scar?"

"Yes, him. Sasha. I'd never been close enough to smell him. But I did tonight."

"And you're not sure what to do."

"I'm not."

"Do you want him?"

Hunter forced himself to think of that. Did he want Sasha? Yes. God, he did. And he wanted more than sex with him. As incredible as it felt, he wanted to talk to Sasha, to find out what he wanted, how to make him happy. He wanted to know everything there was about him. He wanted to make him happy.

And he had no idea how to do that.

He closed his eyes. "Where do I even start with this? I've never romanced anyone. I don't even have to look for people. They come to me."

Michael snorted. "I never thought I'd see you like this. Okay. So you want Sasha."

"Yes." And how much he wanted him was petrifying. "What do I do?"

Michael chuckled. "You'll find a way. He's your mate. As long as you want him and he wants you, everything's going to be okay."

"You think?"

"Yes. Mates find each other for a reason. I'm not saying it's going to be easy, but I do think there's a reason you found him now. You're ready to stop dicking around and fall in love."

Hunter wasn't so sure about that.

Chapter Two

Sasha still felt unsteady when he woke up the day after he'd been so close to Hunter. He'd dreamed of him, and he didn't understand it. He didn't understand anything anymore, and he hated it. He wanted his old, predictable life back—but he knew that wasn't going to happen.

Hunter had wriggled his way under Sasha's skin, and he wasn't leaving.

Sasha rubbed his face and forced himself to get up. It was late, just before lunch, and he needed to eat something before going to work. Nate expected him to be there early so they could give the bar a good clean-up and get everything ready before the Saturday night crowd. The bar would be open until one tomorrow morning, and Sasha wasn't looking forward to it.

He stretched and got out of bed. He *really* needed to get Hunter out of his head, or he wouldn't be able to do much of anything today.

He felt better by the time he was out of the shower, dressed, and on his way to the bar. Hunter was still on his mind, but it was easy to push him to the back of it and focus on the food he was about to eat, especially when he hadn't eaten breakfast. The coffee shop was bustling with people chatting and drinking their coffee, and Sasha got in line, his stomach grumbling at the sight of the sandwiches and pasta salads. He was still trying to decide what he'd eat when someone bumped into him. He turned, smiling when he saw it was Grey, and pulled his hair in front of his face. "Hey."

Grey grinned. Sasha narrowed his eyes at him. He looked like someone who knew something Sasha didn't and who couldn't wait to tell him—or maybe hold it over his head. "Good morning, Sasha."

"What's going on?"

Grey tried to look innocent, but Sasha thought he looked deranged. "I have no idea what you're talking about."

"Of course you don't. Are you staying around for lunch?"

"Yep. Want to eat together?"

They squeezed themselves into a corner table. Their elbows banged together every time they raised them. It felt good to spend time with someone. They were friends, but Sasha was aware he kept everyone at arm's length, including the few friends he had.

"So, anything new?" Grey asked.

He *definitely* was up to something. "No."

"Are you sure?"

"Why don't you just come out with it and ask? What do you want to know?"

Grey put down his fork. "I was just wondering what you think of Hunter."

Sasha swallowed. He wasn't sure how to answer that. He didn't want to tell Grey he seemed to be obsessed with Hunter right now, but he also wanted to know what Grey knew. "I don't know him well enough to think anything about him." And wasn't that the truth.

"I'm sure you have an idea."

Sasha hesitated. He didn't want to offend Grey—Hunter was one of his best friends after all—but he also didn't want to lie. "He's a playboy. He's with a different person every time I see him, and never for long. But I don't have anything against him. Like I said, I don't know him. I don't think we've ever even talked before."

Grey nibbled his lower lip. "He was a playboy, you're

right. Although that word makes him sound like Casanova or something."

"Whatever you call it doesn't matter."

"I guess it doesn't."

"Why *was*? He was with a guy last night." And while Sasha hadn't been in the hallway when said guy had asked Hunter for his number, he hadn't been far, and he'd heard the conversation.

Grey cleared his throat and looked down at his bowl of pasta. "You should talk to him. He's a good guy. I won't deny he likes sex, but that doesn't mean he's going to hurt you. He's loyal."

"I'm not sure why you're telling me this."

"I just don't want you to be closed off to him."

"Again, what are you talking about?"

Grey tapped his fingertips on the table. "Okay. Let's just say you caught his eye."

Sasha went rigid. "I'm not looking for sex."

Grey raised his hands. "I know, I know. That's obvious. But I wasn't talking about that. He's . . . he has a crush on you."

Sasha frowned. "I never noticed anything."

"That's because he has no idea how to behave. You were right when you said he likes sex. That's what he's used to. But he wants more with you, Sasha."

"I don't understand why."

Grey patted Sasha's hand. "You will. Just give him a chance."

Sasha was glad it was time for him to go to work. He wasn't sure what Grey was up to and wasn't sure he wanted to find out. He'd been weird, and Sasha was done with weird. He never wanted his life to get weird again.

Nate was already in the bar when Sasha got there. Sasha smiled, knowing he'd tease him about being late anyway.

Nate lived above the bar, and he often went back upstairs between one task and another. "Nate?" he called out, closing the door.

"I'm in the back room! Just start on the bar, will you?"

"Your wish is my command."

"Fuck off!"

Sasha laughed. He went to put his backpack in the break room but kept his phone in his pocket. No one ever called him, but he was so used to it that he felt naked without it. That, and he liked to play stupid games while he waited for the time to open the bar.

He lost himself in his work, scrubbing the counter down and putting away the glasses that were still in the dishwasher.

Then someone knocked on the door just as Sasha was putting the bottles Nate had brought from the back room on the shelves. He didn't bother looking back. "We're closed!" he yelled.

There was another knock. Sasha huffed and looked back. It couldn't be one of the suppliers, because they used the back door. Most customers knew the bar opened later in the afternoon. Besides, if it was a customer, surely they'd heard Sasha yelling that it was closed.

Who the fuck was it, then?

At the third knock, Sasha put down the bottle in his hand and went to open the door. His glare froze on his face when he found Hunter on the other side of the door. He was holding a bouquet of colorful flowers, and he looked like he wasn't quite sure what to do.

He thrust the flowers into Sasha's hands, and Sasha grabbed them instinctively. He blinked down at them. Not understanding what was going on. "What are you doing here?" he asked. He winced a bit. He could have been a bit nicer, but he was surprised, and that had never agreed with him well.

Hunter rubbed the back of his neck. He shuffled his feet, and he looked so much like a child trying to apologize that Sasha wanted to give him anything he wanted. He was adorable.

"I'm Hunter."

Sasha pressed his lips together. "I know."

"I came by to talk to you. And to bring you flowers."

"They're for me?"

"Yes. I wasn't sure you liked them, or if those flowers are okay. I wanted to do something nice, but I honestly have no idea where to start. Maybe I should have bought chocolate. Do you like chocolate?"

The last time anyone had bought Sasha a gift, it had been Cedric, and this reminded him of his boyfriend. He raised the flowers to his nose and inhaled deeply, the scent of the flowers relaxing him. "I like chocolate. I also like the flowers, though. I just don't understand why you brought them to me?"

Hunter licked his lips. "I told you, I want to talk to you."

"Why?"

"Do you have a little time?"

Sasha looked back. The counter was still full of bottles he needed to put away, and he had to sweep the floors before the bar opened. "Not really."

"Oh. What about later today?"

Sasha wanted to say no, but he also wanted to find out what Hunter wanted from him. He wanted to be close to Hunter, and this was one way to get that. He still didn't know why, but he guessed he was going to find out when they talked. "I have a break later today."

"And we can talk then?"

"If you don't mind that I'll have to eat during our conversation, yes. It's my dinner break. Or you can wait until the next break that's later."

"Your dinner break is fine." He hesitated, then leaned forward and kissed Sasha's cheek. "Thank you."

Sasha touched his cheek and watched Hunter walk away.

What the fuck had just happened?

Hunter had no idea how things had gone. He had to force himself from looking back, even though he knew Sasha had already closed the door. Had Sasha liked the flowers? He hadn't thrown them away or told Hunter to fuck off, so Hunter was cautiously optimistic, but that didn't mean much. Maybe he just liked flowers.

No, the important part was going to be the conversation they'd have later, and Hunter needed to think about what he'd say.

He couldn't go home—he'd managed to sneak out without Nysys noticing, but the Nix would see him if he went back and forth. Besides, he didn't want to hang around in his room most of the afternoon. It was going on four, and that meant he'd only have to wait three hours until he could talk to Sasha.

What was he going to do in the meantime?

He walked to the park. There were a lot of people there, mostly families and teenagers, but he managed to find an empty bench set away from the main paths and sat down. He leaned back and closed his eyes, mumbling to himself.

"What the fuck am I going to tell him? Hey, Sasha, by the way, I know I've fucked anything that moves in the past, but we're mates, and now I only want you?"

"I'm sure you can come up with something better than that," Grey said.

Hunter jerked and glared at him. "What do you want?"

"I was just wondering what you were doing. I saw you

passing by the coffee shop and thought I was going to keep you company. What are you doing here? You came to talk to Sasha?"

"Yeah, but he's working. He said I could come back at seven when he goes on break."

Grey nodded. He sat next to Hunter on the bench, and Hunter knew he wasn't going to like what came out of his mouth next. He never did when Grey looked like a kicked puppy. "What have you done?" he asked, sure Grey *had* done something.

"I had lunch with Sasha."

Shit. Had Sasha told Grey he didn't want anything to do with Hunter? He hadn't looked angry when they'd talked, but how could Hunter be sure? "And?" He couldn't get anything else out.

Grey leaned back and looked at the sky. "He's closed off, Hunter. I don't know what happened to him, and I didn't ask because I doubt he'd tell me. Maybe he'll open up to you, but it's not going to be easy. I'll be honest, I don't think he's going to fall into your arms like the others have, even if you tell him he's your mate."

"I *am* going to tell him. He deserves to know." Even if he didn't want Hunter. After all, it would be Hunter's problem. Sasha was human, so he'd have an easier time letting go if he didn't want him. And Hunter, well, he supposed he could go back to his one-night stands. He could forget Sasha *if* it came to that. They'd only talked once, and even though Hunter's python wanted him so much it would fight Hunter for control, Hunter was confident he'd be able to keep control.

"You're right, he does. And I *do* think that eventually, he'll warm up to you."

"But not right away." Why was Hunter feeling a sense of panic at that thought? He hadn't even wanted a mate until last night, so why was the thought of losing Sasha making it hard to breathe?

"I don't know, Hunter. You'll need to get through his defenses, and that's not going to be easy. I consider myself one of his friends, yet even I don't know anything about his life before he moved to Gillham. But whatever happened, it hurt him, and not a little. It's going to take some work." He paused, and Hunter tensed for what was coming. "You shouldn't start anything with him if you're not serious about him."

Hunter blinked. Had Grey really said that? "Not serious? What do you think I'm going to do, fuck him and dump him? He's my mate, for fuck's sake. Of course I'm serious about him."

Grey raised his hands. "I know, I know. But you have to admit your history isn't the greatest."

"I know, but those people weren't my mates. Sasha is. It's different."

"I know it is. I've just been through this, remember? But Sasha isn't Patrick, and he's wounded. If he gives you a chance, you're going to have to take things slow and tiptoe into this relationship. He looked like he might flee with one wrong word, and we both know you put your foot in your mouth more often than not."

Hunter rubbed his face. Were all relationships this complicated? He hadn't even talked to Sasha yet, and he was terrified of failing. Hell, from what Grey was saying, he was going to fail. He was going to lose Sasha before he was even his.

No. Hunter couldn't freak out. He wouldn't be able to do what he had to do if he did. It would be so much easier to go back home and forget about this.

Hunter's python hissed at him, and he pushed back. He wasn't going to leave. He might not have wanted a mate, but it wasn't like he hated the idea. It was new and foreign, but he knew he'd get used to it.

He'd watched Grey fall in love with Patrick. Grey had gone from a slightly sad, disappointed-in-men guy to someone who was always smiling. Patrick made him happy, and he made Patrick happy. Wasn't that the most important thing? Hunter might have never known that was what he wanted, but he did now. It was weird, but that didn't mean he was going to screw things up.

He wouldn't. "I'll give him all the time he needs, even if I have to wait for years for him to be comfortable with me being his mate."

Grey smiled. "Years?"

"I hope it won't come to that, but it's not like I don't have time."

"You won't be able to have sex all that time."

Hunter shrugged. "That's why I have a right hand. I can probably manage to learn to do it with the left one, too."

Grey rolled his eyes. "Of course you can." He patted Hunter's knee. "But I'm glad you're taking this seriously. You're always so lighthearted, I wasn't sure you could."

"I'm not when I'm working."

"This isn't work."

"Maybe not, but I can focus on this as if it were." Maybe he could make it his objective to bond with Sasha. If he looked at this like a work assignment, he might be able to focus on it instead of panicking.

The thought helped Hunter settle down. He was used to hard work, and this wasn't different—he could deal with it.

"What are your plans, then?" Grey asked.

"I'm going to talk to him. I'll be honest. I'll tell him we're mates and that I'd like him to give me a chance. I'll promise he's going to be the only one for me from now on. I realize it will take him a while to trust me, but I'm ready to wait."

Grey stared at Hunter. "You know, I wasn't sure this was a good idea. I love you, but you're not the most serious guy I know, and I didn't want Sasha to get hurt. This might actually work, though. Patrick told me that he thinks there's a reason you of all people are Sasha's mate. I wasn't sure about it, but the fact that you're taking it seriously makes me rethink it."

Hunter pouted. "I'm not sure if I should be offended that you think so badly of me."

"Not badly. I'm just realistic. There's more to you than what you show the world, though. I have faith in you, and I think you'll be good for Sasha. Maybe having you in his life will help him work out what happened in his past. I want him to be happy."

"And you think *I* can make him happy?" Hunter wanted to believe he could, but the thought that Sasha's happiness depended on him was horrifying. What if he messed up?

"I think you can, yes. You'll probably also make him spitting mad, and he'll want to kill you twice a day, but that's just the way you are. It doesn't mean he won't love you. I do, even though sometimes I want to bash you upside the head."

"You're not making feel better."

"Good. You need to stay on your toes. He's going to make you work for it."

Hunter had never been afraid of hard work.

Sasha checked the time for what had to be the hundredth time in the past half an hour. He ignored Nate's snicker and tried to focus on not breaking any more glasses, but it was hard. All his thoughts—except the one fixed on the time—were on Hunter.

Which reminded him. What time was it? He'd checked his

phone, but his brain hadn't registered the info because it was so focused on Hunter.

Nate laughed out loud as he pushed a beer toward the customer who'd ordered it. "Take your break, Sasha."

"I don't think it's time yet."

"It's only ten minutes to seven, and hopefully you won't manage to break anything else. Go on. The crowd isn't big yet, so I can handle this on my own for a bit." When Sasha didn't move, he gestured toward the hallway. "Go before I change my mind."

Sasha was done waiting. He wasn't sure if Hunter was already there, but he couldn't see him anywhere in the bar. That would give him a little time to wash his hands and face and to check that his hair covered his scar. He felt ridiculous even thinking about making himself presentable for Hunter, but he couldn't deny that was what was going on.

He still didn't understand why. Why was he so drawn to Hunter? And why was Hunter so interested in him? It didn't make sense. Sasha was just a bartender. He looked average—long brown hair, brown eyes, five feet nine, slight built. The only remarkable thing about him was the scars, and he didn't want Hunter to want him for that. He'd never encountered someone who was attracted to scars before, but he supposed anything was possible.

When he came back to the bar area, Hunter was hovering by the counter, looking like he'd rather be anywhere but there—and like he wanted to strangle Nate. Who knew what Nate had told him while Sasha had been away?

Sasha rushed to his side, glaring at Nate again. "Hey, Hunter."

Hunter beamed, and Sasha had a hard time believing that smile was for him. He was tempted to turn around and make sure one of Hunter's past conquests wasn't behind him. "Hey, Sasha. Ready to go?"

Sasha blinked. "Go?"

"Out for dinner."

"But I'm working."

"And I know from reliable sources that you still need to eat."

"That wasn't a reliable source. It was just Nate, and he's being an asshole, like always."

"It *is* your lunch break, though, right?"

Sasha couldn't help but smile. "It is. And no, I haven't eaten yet. I usually grab something from the kitchen."

"I have a better idea, if you're up for it."

"Depends what it is."

Hunter tilted his head toward the door. "Come on."

Following Hunter out of the bar gave Sasha a thrill. His stomach felt like it was filled with butterflies, and while he didn't want to feel that way, he knew he couldn't ignore it.

He liked Hunter, even though he didn't want to. Even though he didn't know why.

Even though it shouldn't be possible.

Hunter led Sasha toward the parking lot. Sasha frowned when he recognized Grey's truck. Hunter reached into the open back and took out a basket. Sasha wasn't sure what he'd expected, but it wasn't that. "What's going on?"

Hunter raised the basket. His cheeks were flushed, and he was adorable. "I thought we could have a picnic."

"A picnic?"

"Yeah. In the park. That way you can get some fresh air, eat, and we can talk. Most people went home, so it's fairly empty."

There was no way Sasha could say no to that. Hunter was flustered and looked like he expected a rejection, and Sasha didn't think that was the sign of someone who didn't care. He didn't know *why* Hunter cared, but he couldn't deny what he was seeing. Maybe talking to him would clarify things because he needed answers. "That sounds good."

Hunter's shoulders slumped in what Sasha thought was relief. "Great. Let's go, then."

Sasha followed Hunter toward the park. He couldn't help but sneak glances at him. He'd never really had a type, and Hunter was the opposite of Cedric, at least physically. Cedric had been on the shorter side, like Sasha, and dark—dark hair, dark eyes, dark complexion, especially during the summer. Hunter, on the other hand, was a blond. He was tall, tall enough that he'd be able to wrap himself around Sasha and make him feel safe.

Sasha shook his head. He needed to keep whatever part of himself that wanted to climb Hunter like a tree under control. "Why did you want to talk?" he asked instead of thinking about how round Hunter's ass was in those jeans he was wearing.

Hunter smiled at him. "Let's wait until we're sitting down, yeah?"

Sasha wanted to say no. He hated waiting, especially when the answers were so close, but what could he do? Luckily for him and his impatience, they didn't go far. The park was almost completely empty, so they found a bench right away. Hunter took a blanket out of the basket and spread it on the bench, waving at Sasha to sit once he was done.

Sash obeyed. He was bemused by the care Hunter had obviously put into this. It was also confusing, because Sasha still didn't understand what Hunter wanted from him. Did he want them to be friends? Sasha doubted he'd be doing this kind of thing for a friend, though. And he knew from observing Hunter that he didn't put this kind of effort into finding someone to have sex with, so he didn't think that was it, either. "What did you want to talk about?" he asked once he was seated.

Instead of answering, Hunter offered him a soda and a plastic container full of sandwiches. Sasha recognized an evasive technique when he saw one, and he decided to wait before asking again. Hunter didn't seem to be ready to talk, and Sasha could understand that.

They ate in silence, but it wasn't awkward. It was heavy with unasked questions and unsaid explanations, though, so it was a bit uncomfortable. Sasha both wanted to run back to the bar and never talk to Hunter again and to climb into Hunter's lap and say fuck it to talking.

He still wasn't sure which one he was going to do.

He helped Hunter put away the empty containers when they were done. They bagged the rubbish, too, and put everything back into the basket. Sasha had been nervous about talking, and he still was, but he felt better. They'd spent twenty minutes together, and he'd relaxed. He still wanted to know what was going on, though.

He leaned back against the bench and looked at Hunter. "Ready to talk?"

Hunter gave him a deprecating smile. "Not really. But I have to, don't I?"

"Well, we could decide to talk tomorrow, but I would think about this until then, and I have to be able to focus on my work tonight. Nate is going to start taking money out of my paycheck if I continue breaking glasses."

Hunter frowned. "Do you break a lot of them?"

"Not usually."

"So it's because of me?"

Sasha sighed. "Not exactly. But I can't deny you unsettle me."

"Why? If you can tell me, of course."

Sasha didn't *want* to tell him, but it might help Hunter to finally spit out what he had to say. Whatever it was, it had to be big for him to be so hesitant. Sasha didn't know him well, but he'd observed him often enough to know it wasn't like him. "I'm not sure. There's something about you. That's all I can say. You make me nervous, yet I want to spend more time with you. I know it doesn't make sense, but that's how I feel, and I wish I understood it."

Hunter rubbed the back of his neck. "I can explain why you feel that way."

"You can? Is that what you want to talk about?"

"Yeah. I'm not sure how to say this, though. I've never done it before, obviously."

"Just say it. You're making me even more nervous." But Sasha couldn't deny it was thrilling to see Hunter so flustered. He knew he was the one making it happen, as incredible as it sounded.

Hunter nodded. "All right. I'll just say it, then." He looked straight at Sasha. "We're mates. *You* are my mate."

That was *not* what Sasha had expected.

Hunter held his breath and waited. He couldn't look away from Sasha. He was trying to read every single movement Sasha was making, every expression that appeared on his face.

He couldn't read Sasha, no matter how hard he tried.

He swallowed and forced himself to stay still and quiet, to give Sasha time to process the bomb he'd just let explode.

He wished Sasha would at least smile, though. It would make him feel better and like he maybe had a chance with him.

Sasha cocked his head. "Your mate?" he finally asked.

Hunter licked his lips. "Yes."

"Are you sure?"

"Yes. I realized it when we were in the hallway the other day. I'd never been close enough to you before."

"Is it possible that you smelled someone else? Maybe someone who'd passed through the hallway before me?"

"No." Hunter wasn't sure why Sasha seemed to want him to be wrong, but it made his heart hurt.

He'd never opened himself to anyone the way he was doing with Sasha, and he was only doing it because Sasha was his mate. He *should* want Hunter. Hunter might understand he didn't if he was a terrible person, but he didn't think he was. Right?

He might have had a lot of hookups, and okay, he hadn't exactly been nice to some of the people he'd had sex with when they'd asked for his number, but that didn't make him a bad guy. A conceited one, possibly. But he'd never wanted to hurt anyone, and he knew those people hadn't thought twice about him since then.

Sasha leaned back against the bench. He wrapped his arms around himself as if Hunter had dealt him a blow. It was clear he wasn't happy about this. He was trying to find a way out, and Hunter's heart felt like it was in pieces. If this was what love felt like, then he didn't ever want to feel it again, and he was glad he hadn't let himself feel it for anyone before Sasha.

"I don't know what to say," Sasha murmured.

Hunter shook himself. Sasha might not look happy about this, but that didn't mean he wouldn't change his mind, or even that he hated it. Maybe he was just shocked. Maybe he wasn't sure how to react to it because he hadn't expected it.

Or maybe he didn't want to be bonded to Hunter for the rest of his life.

No. Hunter couldn't think that way. Even though the only thing he wanted to do was to leave and go curl up in his bed to hide away from the world. Sasha was his only chance at having a mate, at knowing what being bonded meant and felt like. He wasn't going to give up easily. It was no doubt going to hurt, but he was used to pain, although usually, it was physical rather than emotional. "Just tell me how you feel. It doesn't matter if it's bad. I can take it. Then we can start working things out."

Sasha shook his head. The movement made his hair slide to the side, exposing the half of his face he always kept hidden. Hunter ached to kiss it, to show him that he was beautiful even with the scar and that it didn't make him weak, pitiful, or whatever bullshit other people might think.

"What do you want?"

Hunter shook his head. "We're not talking about me right now."

"But we are. This is something that affects both of us, isn't it?"

"Yes, but—"

"But nothing. I don't think you've ever been in a relationship. Have you?"

Dammit. Hunter didn't want to talk about himself. He wanted to talk about Sasha and what he wanted. But he couldn't say no to his mate. He doubted he'd ever be able to. "No, I haven't."

"Why not?"

Hunter wasn't sure how to answer that. He wasn't even sure he *had* an answer to that question. "I don't know. I've never felt the need. None of the people I've been with made me feel like I'd want to spend more than a few hours with them."

"Are you going to say I'm different?"

"Yeah, because you are. You're my mate. That means something, both to me and my python."

Sasha blinked. "You're a python shifter?"

That was something Hunter had no problem talking about. "Yep. I'll show you sometime."

"Don't change the subject, Hunter. I asked what you want

from us. From me."

Hunter huffed, but Sasha deserved to know. "Well, you know what a mate is."

Sasha rolled his eyes. "Of course I do. I'd have to live on Mars not to. I know you won't get a second one, and that you and your . . . python will want me for a while if I say no."

Hunter's heart stopped beating. "Is that what you're going to do?"

"Say no? No. But honestly, I'm not sure what I want. I never thought I'd be in this situation."

Hunter rubbed his palms on his thighs. "I understand this is something big. It is for me, too."

"But you've known all your life that your mate was out there."

"I've also known all my life that I might never find him or her. That's why I never gave it much thought. I'm still young even by human standards, so by shifters standards, I'm little more than a baby."

Sasha pressed his lips together, but Hunter could see he wanted to smile. Good. At least Hunter could make him smile. That was something. He hoped he could make him feel other things, too—and not annoyance like most people seemed to feel around him. He was an acquired taste, and not everyone enjoyed that.

"All right, so you've never thought about finding your mate and settling down. But you realized I was your mate last night, right? That's why you kept staring." Sasha paused and wrinkled his nose. "At least this explains why I haven't been able to stop thinking about you."

That was good. Sasha was thinking about Hunter. It was better than nothing, and it was a start. "The same goes for me."

"All right, but you still haven't told me what you want.

You didn't expect to meet your mate. Now that you have, what do you want?"

"You're not going to let this go, are you?"

"I don't think I should."

Hunter sighed. "All right. Like I said before, I'm not sure what I want, but I do know that I won't get another mate, and while some people think I'm an idiot, I'm not so stupid that I'd renounce you."

"So you want us to bond."

"Yeah. Not right away, though. I understand that we don't know each other, and I can tell there's some part of you that's wary of me, or maybe of the situation. I don't know, and it doesn't matter. But I thought we could start as friends, maybe? Get to know each other, go on dates. We'll go as slow or fast as you want, of course. And then maybe in the future, we could bond, if we both want that."

"*You* want it, don't you?"

Hunter shrugged, hoping he looked as uncaring as he was trying to look. He didn't want Sasha to think whichever option was good with him, but he also didn't want to show him how much he'd be hurt if Sasha decided he didn't want to be with him.

He couldn't believe how much meeting Sasha had already changed him. He'd never even thought about settling down with one person in his life, and now there he was, trying to convince Sasha that it was what they should do. He wasn't sure what else to say to convince him, though. He'd promised they could start as friends and possibly progress to more. He'd told Sasha he'd give him as much time as he needed.

He knew they would fall in love if Sasha gave them a chance. They were mates, and that meant something. It meant they were perfect for each other, that Sasha was the only person who could stand being with Hunter for long, and that Hunter was the only person who could love Sasha the way he wanted and deserved.

But that would come later, and only if they were open to it. If Sasha decided he'd rather be without Hunter, then he'd go back to his life, and Hunter would always feel like there was a Sasha-shaped hole in his life. He'd watch him from afar—probably in a creepy way because come on, he was who he was—but he'd leave him alone "Sasha?" Hunter's voice was hoarser than he wanted it to be, but there was nothing he could do about it.

"I need to think," Sasha said, getting up.

Hunter felt like he was losing him already, and he hadn't even had him, not really. "Sasha, please."

Sasha shook his head. "I'm not saying no. But I'm not saying yes, either. I just need time to think."

"Of course." Hunter took out the piece of paper where he'd written his number earlier. "Take this, and call me anytime, even if it's only to ask a question. I truly want you to be comfortable with this. Take your time. I'll wait as long as you need me to."

Chapter Three

Sasha realized he's been staring at the donuts instead of getting in line for coffee. He wasn't sure how long he'd been there, but from the stares, it had been a while.

He hated this. He hated that he couldn't stop thinking — obsessing — about Hunter. He hated — Hunter.

He sighed and rubbed his eyes. That wasn't true. He didn't hate Hunter. He didn't have a reason to hate him.

But he couldn't stop thinking about him.

Sighing, he got in line for coffee, but his thoughts drifted to Hunter again. Their picnic had been four days ago, and Sasha hadn't stopped thinking about what they'd talked about.

He still hadn't decided, though. He didn't even know where to start.

He didn't want to tell Hunter he didn't want him. That would be a lie. He *did* want Hunter, more than he'd thought he'd ever want anyone again, but he'd already been through this with Cedric, and he wasn't sure he'd have the strength to do it again.

He'd lost Cedric. He still had nightmares about that day. He felt like a part of him had died with Cedric, and he'd never gotten it back. But meeting Hunter was making something in Sasha's chest stir, and he wasn't sure he wanted that to happen. What if he lost Hunter, too? What if he opened up to him, let himself fall in love with him, and lost him? Hunter's job was dangerous. He was an enforcer, and they dealt with other shifters, shifters that had gone mad, shifters who were breaking the law. A lot of things could go badly, and what would happen to Sasha if they did? He'd be alone again. He'd have lost again.

He didn't think he was strong enough to go through it.

"You're day-dreaming," a voice said next to him.

Sasha yelped and jumped. He looked up, realizing the line had gone on, several people walking around him as he lost himself in thoughts of Hunter again.

He groaned and glared at Grey. "What do you want?"

Grey gently pushed him forward. "To get coffee. Isn't that what you want, too?"

Sasha sighed. Grey hadn't done anything to him. He shouldn't snap at him. "Yes, it is."

"Come on, then."

Sasha was glad that Grey waited until they both had their coffee and were sitting at a table to ask, "So, you're the reason Hunter's been moping around, aren't you?"

Sasha leaned back in his chair and rubbed his face. He was tired—even his nights were full of Hunter's presence, and that didn't help him sleep. "I don't know."

"Yeah, you do. Want to tell me what happened? I asked Hunter, but he said it was private and that he wouldn't talk about it unless you were okay with it."

Sasha didn't particularly want to talk, not even with Grey, but he couldn't deny it was tempting. Grey had a mate. He knew what Sasha was going through, at least in part. Maybe he could help. He certainly knew Hunter better than Sasha did. "Do you think he's changed?" he asked.

Grey frowned. "You mean if he's really going to stick with you for the rest of your life?"

"Yes." That was one of Sasha's worries. The biggest one was that Sasha might lose him because he'd die, but what if he fell in love with someone else? Or, more probably, what if one man wasn't enough for him? What if he wanted more . . . variety in his bed?

"I don't think that's going to be a problem. I know Hunter. While it's true that he's used to having a lot of lovers, and I'm using that word lightly because let's face it, he didn't have feelings for any of the people he fucked, you're different. You're his mate, and he's loyal. If he gives you his promise, if you two start a relationship, he won't break it. Hell, he hasn't been with anyone since he found you. Even though you haven't said yes, you're his mate, and that fact is enough to form a certain kind of bond between the two of you. Until you tell him you don't want him, he'll respect that, and even after that happens, I doubt he'll be able to forget you anytime soon."

"You think I'm going to say no?"

Grey arched a brow. "Aren't you? I mean, it's been days, right? You haven't even called him back, or texted him."

"That doesn't mean I've made my decision."

Grey nodded. "I get it, you know. It's hard to think about spending the rest of your life with a guy you barely know."

"You didn't have a problem when you met Patrick."

"You're right, I didn't. But I don't think we have much in common when it comes to our past, do we?"

Sasha bit his lower lip. He hadn't talked about Cedric to anyone. He wasn't sure he wanted to, even though he liked Grey. "I don't know."

"I've never lost anyone. My family loves me, and they don't care that I'm with a man. I have friends and a life I love. A job I enjoy. But what about you? I've never seen you with anyone. You talk to me, but it's clear you hide a lot of yourself. I don't know what happened to you, but I can tell it was bad, so I understand why this is hard for you."

Sasha looked down. He couldn't see pity in Grey's eyes. Not in his. "You're right. I did lose someone."

"You loved him."

"Yes."

"And now what? You're afraid you might lose Hunter, too?"

"In part."

"Well, no one can promise you won't."

"He has a dangerous job."

"So do I, and so does Patrick. It's a risk we take because it's worth it."

"What would you do if something happened to Patrick today, or tomorrow?"

"I'd be broken. But I wouldn't be sorry I let him into my life and loved him. I would have lost much more than I stand to lose if something does happen to him. I wouldn't have known his love and how he makes me feel."

Sasha wasn't sure he shared that view. Some days, he wished he'd never met Cedric, or that he hadn't agreed to go on that first date with him. Cedric might not have died if he hadn't, and even if he had, Sasha wouldn't have been in so much pain. It was easy for Grey to talk about it, but Sasha had gone through it, and he didn't want it to happen again.

He rubbed his face. "I don't know."

Grey patted his hand. "I get it. And you don't have to make any decision now. But please, at least text him. I got enough calls from his friends. They're worried about him. I am, too. I know what's going on, but he's not himself. He's worried about you, and not only because he wants you to say yes."

"He talked to you?"

"A bit. He hates that he's making you choose."

Sasha bit his lower lip. He might not know what he wanted from Hunter, but he didn't want him to be hurt. "Would a text do?"

Grey grinned. "Yes. He's really just worried that he's pushing too hard or that maybe you've already made your decision and that you don't want to tell him you don't want him in your life."

"I don't know how long it's going to take me to decide."

"Take your time, but nothing is going to change, Sasha. Things will still be the same, tomorrow, in a week, or in a year. I understand that you're afraid and that you want to be sure, but think about where this leaves Hunter. He's in limbo when it comes to his personal life. He's waiting for you, and he can't move forward until he knows what you want. So if you think you're going to ultimately say no, then don't string him along. It would be cruel, and I know you're not a cruel guy."

Sasha closed his eyes. He didn't want Hunter to be hurt. He knew he had to make his decision, and that he'd have to do it soon. It would be easier for everyone if he didn't drag it out.

He hated that the knowledge made choosing even harder, though, and that it showed him how much he already cared for Hunter. He suspected there would be no kicking Hunter out of his life, whether he liked it or not—and whether he chose to be with Hunter or not.

Hunter stared at the ceiling so he wouldn't stare at his phone. He hoped it would make it ring, or even ping, but of course, it didn't. It wasn't like the water that didn't boil if you looked at it—it was Sasha who didn't want to talk to him. He wouldn't call even if Hunter tried to forget about him.

Hunter hoped that would change. It had only been four days after all, and he'd seen how wary Sasha was of the situation. He wasn't sure why, since Sasha hadn't told him, but he wasn't as blind as most people thought he was, and he could put two and two together. Sasha had been hurt, and he wasn't sure he wanted to risk his heart again. It wasn't something Hunter could understand, but he respected it.

That didn't mean he didn't want his mate to want to be with him. He'd even accept being friends if Sasha was more comfortable with that. But dammit, he needed Sasha to call.

Hunter rubbed his face with both hands. He could call Sasha, but he knew better. It was his first instinct, and when it came to his instincts, he didn't trust them when it came to relationships. He knew better than to follow them and push Sasha too hard too fast and possibly lose him.

He wanted to, though. He didn't understand why he was so obsessed with Sasha. He was his mate, but did that explain it? How could Hunter have gone from not caring for the people he had sex with to wanting to have sex with the same man for the rest of his life? He knew it was because Sasha was his mate, and he didn't mind that fact, but it boggled his mind. Who would have thought he'd change his tune so much? Who would have thought he'd care for one man so much that he hadn't even thought about having sex with someone else since he'd realized Sasha was his mate? Finding your mate really changed your life, even when he didn't want anything to do with you.

Hunter sighed and closed his eyes. He needed to stop thinking about Sasha. It wasn't helping. The only thing it did was make Hunter feel like he'd never be happy again, and he knew that wasn't true. Sasha might be his mate, but his happiness didn't depend on him. He had a life away from Sasha, and while it didn't feel the way it had before — as if Hunter was a different man now — it was good enough.

Something heavy fell onto Hunter's stomach. He yelped and folded himself in half, breathless and hurting — and glaring at Nysys, who was sitting on his stomach.

Hunter pushed him off, and he wasn't even sorry that Nysys fell to the floor. "What the fuck?"

Nysys glared from the floor and made a show of rubbing his ass. "Why did you push me off?"

"Why did you shimmer right on top of me?"

"I didn't mean to do that. It's not my fault you were spread out on the couch like a pillow."

"Didn't Dominic tell you not to shimmer around the house?"

Nysys shrugged. "He's not here to see me do it."

Hunter wasn't surprised that he didn't care. He *was* surprised that he hadn't heard other people complaining about it, though. Nysys had the tendency to shimmer into places people didn't want him in, like into bedrooms at night.

Hunter flopped back on the couch and waved. "Whatever. Just do what you came here to do."

Nysys moved to his knees and leaned so close to Hunter that Hunter could feel his breath on his cheek—he'd just had coffee. *Ugh.* "What's wrong?"

"Nothing."

Nysys arched a brow. "Really? Why aren't you fucking your mate right now, then?"

Trust Nysys to go straight to the point and break whatever stood in his way to do it—even Hunter's feelings. "Because he's busy."

"Busy doing what? I remember when Morin and I first bonded—"

"We haven't bonded. Remind me again, how long did it take you to bond with Morin?"

Nysys glared. "None of your business."

"Then stay out of mine."

Nysys pouted. "I was just trying to help."

Hunter sighed. He didn't want to hurt Nysys. He knew he was sticking his nose into this because he cared, just like he'd done the other day. After all, it was partially thanks to him that Hunter had decided to talk to Sasha. He was still in the same position, but that wasn't Nysys' fault. "I know. Sorry if I snapped."

Nysys sat back, crossing his legs. He was wearing jeans and a pink t-shirt. His feet were bare, and his nails were painted green. Hunter smiled. "The green of your nails doesn't go with the t-shirt."

Nysys flipped him the bird. "Unless you want me to shimmer into your bed at two in the morning, I'd shut up."

"No need to take out the big guns. I won't comment on your clothing anymore."

"Good. Because you're wearing your enforcer uniform even though you're not working."

"I trained earlier."

"And you showered. Couldn't you put on normal clothes?"

"Couldn't you?"

Nysys whacked Hunter on the arm. "Shut it, or you'll find yourself with dead fish in your bed."

Since Nysys *had* done that to someone, Hunter wasn't going to risk it. "Sorry."

Nysys sighed. "Never mind. What's bothering you, Hunter? Tell your uncle Nysys."

"You're not my uncle. We're not even related." *Thank God for small mercies.*

"But I'm older than you. Come on. You know I'm not going to let this go until you talk to me."

And he was only going to get pushier. "I talked with Sasha the other day."

"Mmm. I take it it didn't go well?"

"Not really."

"Did he reject you?"

"Not in those words." Hunter wasn't hopeful, though. He did want to give Sasha all the time he needed, but Sasha's reaction had been enough to tell Hunter he wasn't thrilled.

He hadn't told Hunter why, but he didn't need to.

"I'm sure you're making this worse than it sounds. Come on, talk to me."

Hunter supposed he might as well. Grey had texted him to tell him he'd talked to Sasha and to offer Hunter a shoulder to cry on if he needed one. Hunter had declined because he didn't want Grey to feel like he was stuck in the middle, but Nysys was neutral. "He wanted time."

"Time to think?"

"Yes."

"About what? If he wants to bond with you?"

"If he wants to be with me at all."

Nysys grimaced. "Got it. So he needs to think about this. He's human, right? So maybe he just needs to wrap his mind around it? He probably didn't expect to be a mate. Most humans aren't, and the thought of suddenly finding out you're supposed to spend the next hundred and something years with someone is daunting."

"I realize that. It's why I told him he could take as long as he needed to think."

"Then why do you look like someone killed your dog?"

"I don't have a dog. And because he hasn't even texted. I understand needing time, but shouldn't he at least want to get to know me? How can he make this kind of decision if he doesn't even know me? We could at least start with being friends, you know?"

"I think he's scared."

Hunter rolled on his side and faced Nysys. "Of what? Of spending the rest of his life with me?"

"Maybe, although since you're not that bad of a guy, I doubt that's it. But something is holding him back. Maybe he doesn't want to fall in love. Maybe the bond scares him. Maybe he doesn't like your face."

Hunter grunted and tried to kick Nysys, but Nysys

caught his ankle and pushed his leg back. "You're not helping," Hunter pointed out.

"What I mean is, if he's scared of something, maybe you *should* push a bit. Fear can be paralyzing. It's so much easier to stand back and wait for the universe to make a decision for you, or in this case, for you to decide you don't want to wait anymore and to move on to another person."

Hunter sat up. "I'd never do that."

"But you will if he decides he doesn't want you. Right?"

"I don't want to think about that." For fuck sake, Hunter had just met him. He wasn't already thinking of an alternative.

"I know. He might not. He might be waiting for you to decide for him. It would be easier."

"I promised him I wouldn't push. I don't want to break that promise, not yet." And he prayed that what Nysys was saying wasn't true.

Sasha dumped the ice into the freezer and closed it. He turned to the dishwasher and noticed the cycle was done, so he decided to put away the glasses in it. The mindless work wasn't good for his mind, though. He was still thinking about—what else—Hunter, and more specifically, the talk he'd had with Grey.

Grey seemed to think that having loved and lost was better than not feeling, but Sasha wasn't so sure about that, and the fact that Grey hadn't lost anyone made him think that maybe he was the one who was right. It *would* be easier to shield himself and push Hunter away. That way, he wouldn't be hurt if he lost him.

He turned around to put away one of the glasses and screamed. His first instinct was to throw the glass at the pink-haired guy who was suddenly standing on the other side of the counter, but he disappeared before the glass could hit him. The glass crashed on the floor, breaking into a thousand pieces.

The pink-haired guy reappeared on Sasha's side of the counter, his hands raised. "Don't throw anything else please. I get enough of that at home."

"Who the fuck are you?" Sasha *was* tempted to throw another glass at him, or maybe even a bottle—a full one so it would hurt.

"My name is Nysys."

"You could be Santa Claus, and I wouldn't care. Get out. The bar is still closed. And we don't appreciate Nix shimmering in. Use the door like everyone else."

Nysys cocked his head. "You're rude."

"I'm not the only one. The door's that way."

Instead of leaving like Sasha had hoped he would, Nysys leaned his hip against the counter and crossed his arms over his chest. He looked Sasha up and down as if he were examining him, and Sasha had to suppress the need to wriggle. Who the fuck was this guy?

He didn't think he'd ever seen him around town, or even in the bar. He would remember him. Not only was his hair bright pink, but he was tattooed and pierced. There was no way he'd be able to hide, even in a crowd, and Sasha had learned to observe since he'd started this job, just in case.

"Why don't you want Hunter?" Nysys asked.

Sasha blinked. "I'm sorry?"

Nysys eyed the counter. He ran his fingers on top of it, then hopped and settled there, looking at ease. "Hunter. You haven't called him."

Why was everyone sticking their noses into this? "What's it to you?"

"He's my friend, and I don't like him being so down. I get that you haven't made your decision yet, although let me tell you, I think you're being stupid, but you could at least text him."

Sasha briefly closed his eyes and took a deep breath. He couldn't break another glass, and he was already going to have to pick up enough glass. "I don't care who you are. This isn't your business."

"Yes, it is. Hunter is my friend. I care for him. I want him to be happy. If you don't want him, tell him. He deserves at least that."

Sasha's hackles rose. "Who said I don't want him?" he asked before he could think about it.

"Uh, you? Your behavior? I mean, you haven't even *texted* him. I text my mate all the time."

"I don't care what you do."

"Maybe not, but *I* care what *you* do. Come on. What's the problem? You think Hunter is going to sleep around on you?"

"What? What do you—"

"Because he won't. I know he couldn't keep it in his pants until now, but you're not just another guy. You're his mate. He hasn't had sex since he met you, which might be one of the reasons he's so grumpy, actually. And he won't have sex with anyone else until you tell him you don't want him."

That was what Grey had said, too. Sasha wanted to believe him, and this Nysys guy. The fact that they were both talking about Hunter in a positive way was good, right? He wouldn't have such loyal friends if he was an asshole.

But that wasn't the only problem Sasha had with him. It wasn't even the main one. He didn't know Hunter, but he wasn't going to reject him because of his past. No, the main reason he was staying away was that he knew Hunter wouldn't leave him, that he'd be there for him if he decided to do this.

And *that* was scarier than him cheating. Because what if

Sasha let himself fall in love again?

"I don't care who he had sex with in the past," Sasha said through gritted teeth.

"Good. You shouldn't. They didn't mean anything. What is it, then? He's not handsome enough for you?"

"What are you talking about?"

"There *has* to be a reason you don't want him."

"Again, I never said I didn't want him."

"You haven't, but your actions speak loudly, more so than your words. Would you rather have a rich mate?"

Sasha wanted to strangle the guy, and to make it as painful as possible. "I don't care how much money Hunter has, not any more than I care about who he had sex with in the past."

"Mmm, money isn't a problem, then, and you said you find him sexy."

"I never said that." But it was true. Hunter was one of the most gorgeous men Sasha had ever seen.

Nysys peered at Sasha. "Do you think you're not good-looking enough for him, then? Because I don't think that scar is ugly. It gives your face character. It's interesting."

And it was the reminder of the worst moment in Sasha's life.

He reached up and made sure his hair covered the scar. "Can we not talk about that?"

"Of course. We can talk about why you don't want Hunter."

"Again with this? Who said I didn't want him?"

Nysys arched a brow.

Sasha wasn't going to get an answer, and he didn't need one. He sighed. He didn't know this guy, and he wasn't sure he should trust him, but he could tell he wouldn't get rid of him unless he talked. "I'm scared, all right?"

"Of Hunter? Because he won't hurt you. He's an enforcer,

but that doesn't mean he beats people up when he's off the job."

"I know that, and it's not what I meant."

"You don't want to fall in love with him because of his job."

That wasn't exactly it, but Sasha wasn't about to tell this Nysys guy the entire reason. "Yeah, that's it. What if he gets hurt on the job, or worse? What am I going to do then? We're mates, so if we bond, I'll know if he gets hurt."

"Doesn't that go for humans, too? You're human, right?" Sasha nodded. "Right. So when two humans decide to be together, to get married, they're taking the risk that they might lose each other."

"But they're not enforcers. They don't have a job that puts them in so much danger."

"What about police officers? Or military people? Besides, having a risky job isn't the only way to die. We all could get run over by a bus or a truck any time, right? Or we could have a car accident. Well, I couldn't, since I shimmer everywhere, but you get what I mean."

"Are you supposed to be encouraging? Because it's not working."

Nysys waved Sasha's words away. "What I was trying to say is that we could all die tomorrow, so if we followed your reasoning, we should all hide away and not love anyone, friends or boyfriends, or mates. We should all find a cave in the mountains and stay there."

Sasha rubbed his face. He knew what Nysys was saying was true, but how did he get over the fear? Over the *terror* that if he said yes to Hunter, even to only be friends, he wouldn't get hurt again?

Nysys reached out and patted Sasha's head as if he were a puppy. "I know it's scary. It took me a while to realize all this when I met my mate. I was trying to prove something when that happened, and I kept the fact that we were mates to myself for a while. I resisted the pull. But look at us now. We've been bonded for years, and we've been happy for just as long. You could have that, too. You can't live with the fear that something bad is going to happen. That wouldn't be a life. It would hold you back from everything that's good in this world." He smiled. "Just think about it, okay? No one said you had to choose now. But think."

And with one last wave, he shimmered away, leaving Sasha staring at the counter like an idiot.

Hunter wasn't moping anymore. He'd changed clothes after Nysys had badgered him for wearing his uniform, and instead of staying in his bedroom, he'd gone to the kitchen the enforcers shared. And he didn't regret it. He hadn't thought he was up for company, but it made him feel better. Even if Sasha ultimately decided he didn't want him, he wouldn't be alone. He'd always have his friends and his teammates. It would hurt, but he'd make it through. He was sure of it.

"Hey. I was starting to wonder if you'd quit the job," Michael said as he flopped into the chair next to Hunter.

Hunter pushed the carrots he'd been peeling toward Michael. "Justin needs those for dinner. Help me."

Michael chuckled. "You don't even bother making it sound like a request, do you?"

"That's because it's not. You know how Justin gets when we don't listen to him."

Michael shuddered. "I don't want to have to face his furry half again."

"No one does. Get to work, foxy."

They were only halfway through the pile of carrots when Sarah walked in. From the look on her face, it was obvious the team had been called out for a mission.

Hunter sighed and put down his carrot. He'd always loved his job, and he was still eager to help, but he was wary of leaving right now. What if Sasha decided he wanted to talk to him and he wasn't there? He wouldn't be able to bring his phone with him, and some missions lasted for weeks at a time.

"Team. Gather around," Sarah said, her voice serious.

The enforcers who didn't belong to the team gave them space at the table where Hunter and Michael were sitting, so they stayed where they were. Sarah stayed on her feet like she always did when she was briefing them. Hunter fingered his cell phone on the table and wondered if he'd have the time to call Sasha, or if he should. He still wasn't sure if he should take Nysys' advice of pushing Sasha to at least be friends. Maybe having to leave wouldn't be a bad thing. Hunter wouldn't be able to give in and call Sasha, and Sasha would have the time he needed to make a decision.

"All right," Sarah said when they were all seated. "Quick briefing, then I want all of you to get ready. We're leaving in fifteen minutes. We're going to Brazil, in the rainforest. There have been reports of people using the place to produce that drug that's been killing shifters. They might be members of the Beasts, and even if they're not, there's a good probability that they have at the very least contact with them. The council is investigating more deeply, and they'll send me updates as needed. Our job is to observe and possibly neutralize once the council gives us the go-ahead. We're expecting around ten to fifteen men, all of them armed to the teeth. There could be more, so keep your eyes open. Pryderi will shimmer us there as soon as we're all ready. You have fifteen minutes."

That was their signal. The team members got up from their chairs as one and headed toward the bedrooms. Everyone was going to change and call who they needed to call—

their boyfriend or girlfriend, their parents, whoever would miss them if something happened to them on the mission.

Hunter should be calling Sasha, but he wasn't going to.

He'd promised he wouldn't push, and whatever Nysys thought, now wasn't the time to do it. Maybe when he came back, depending on how long he was gone. But it had only been four days, even though they felt like the longest days in Hunter's life, so it was too soon. Besides, Hunter didn't want Sasha to think he had to do something just because Hunter was being sent on a job.

He couldn't leave without saying anything, though, just in case Sasha decided to call him. Once he was dressed — again — in his uniform, he sat on his bed and tried to compose a message that would tell Sasha he cared without being too overbearing or clingy.

He should start with hello, right?

Hey, Sasha. I don't know if you saved my number on your phone, but this is Hunter. I hope you're doing okay.

Hunter erased that last sentence. He did hope Sasha was okay, but it sounded too stiff, not at all like him. He grinned to himself. Well, in some situations . . .

He shook his head. He needed to get his mind out of the gutter and focus.

I just wanted to let you know that my team is being sent on a mission to Brazil. I won't have my phone with me, but I don't want you to worry. I've been on this kind of mission plenty of times, and I've always come home in one piece.

Was that too morbid? He wanted to reassure Sasha, not make him think about him in pieces.

He canceled that *come home in one piece* bit and wrote, *been fine* instead.

I'll call you when I'm back. If you need anything, call Grey. He'll be able to help you or put you in contact with the council.

Hunter reread what he'd written. It wasn't exactly a love poem, but it would do. It was enough to tell Sasha what was happening and hopefully reassure him.

Someone banged on his door. "Hunter? Move your ass. Sarah is waiting for us," Michael yelled through the door.

For the first time, Hunter didn't want to go. He might not have done anything but mope on the couch during the past four days, but at least he'd been close to Sasha, even with a three-hour drive between them. But now he'd be in freaking Brazil, and if Sasha looked for him, he wouldn't find him. Was this what all the mated enforcers went through every time they went on a mission? Like they were abandoning their mate?

"Hunter!" Michael called out again.

Hunter couldn't keep wasting time. He sent the text and hoped it would be good enough. He turned his phone off and left it in his nightstand drawer. Then he followed Michael downstairs.

Everyone else was already gathered in the room they used to shimmer in and out. Hunter ignored the amused and annoyed glances he got and focused on Sarah.

"All right, people. Pryderi, take Lucy, Justin, and Haley ahead. I'll come, too. Hunter, Michael, he'll be right back for you."

Hunter and Michael nodded. The others disappeared, and Hunter tried to relax. This wasn't any different from any other mission. He'd be far away from Sasha, but maybe that would help Sasha realize he wanted him in his life. Not that he needed Hunter to be in Brazil to know what it was like to be without him, since they hadn't seen each other in four days, but Hunter hoped that Sasha felt the bond and that the distance would make him realize Hunter was worth giving him a chance. He didn't even care if Sasha just wanted to be friends for years, as long as he wanted him in his life.

"You okay?" Michael asked.

Hunter forced himself to smile. "Of course."

"Are you sure? You don't look like you want to go. You're usually bouncing around when we're sent on a mission."

Hunter shrugged. "I don't know."

"Yeah, I don't believe that. But it's okay. Sarah said we were going to have to observe for a while, right? There'll be plenty of time to get this out of you."

Hunter smiled. "So sure you'll manage that?"

"Hell, yes. I'm one of the best interrogators on the team, and I know you've been hiding something from me."

"It's just . . . complicated. You know, with Sasha. I don't want to talk about it."

Michael rolled his eyes. "Isn't *everything* complicated? Everything worth fighting for anyway."

Hunter supposed he was right—and wrong. Hunter's relationship with Sasha appeared complicated at first sight, but if one went deep, it wasn't. They were mates. If they had the chance, they'd fall in love, and they'd be bonded thanks to that. It might take Sasha a bit to decide that was what he wanted, but Hunter had to have faith in him and in the bond they already shared. They hadn't finished the bond yet, and they might not for a while, but it was there, and Hunter refused to believe it didn't mean anything.

Chapter Four

Sasha felt his phone vibrating in his jeans pocket and almost dropped the two bottles of beer he was holding. He managed to put them on the counter in front of the customer, smiled at her, and turned around, taking his phone out, praying to see he had a text, or better yet, a missed call.

He didn't. His phone hadn't vibrated—he'd imagined it.

He sighed and put his phone back. He ignored Nate's gaze as he went back to work, forcing himself to smile at the customers and answer their questions. He couldn't bring himself to chat with them, though, not today, not when he felt like something was tightening around his chest, cutting off his breathing.

Fear.

Not for himself—he had nothing to be scared about, especially not right now since he was at work. No, he was terrified for Hunter.

It had been three days. Three days since Sasha had gotten Hunter's text telling him Hunter was leaving on a mission. Sasha had called as soon as he'd seen it, but it had been too late. Hunter's phone had already been off. He'd called Grey, then, and Grey had told him it was normal and that no one could be sure how long the mission was going to last. He'd also told Sasha not to worry, but Sasha had already known it was a moot suggestion. He'd started worrying as soon as he'd gotten the text and he hadn't stopped yet.

What if Hunter got hurt? What if he died? He'd do so

without even talking to Sasha again, and it would be Sasha's fault. Why hadn't he at least texted, dammit?

He sighed and rubbed his face. There was nothing he could do about that now. He was going to have to wait for Hunter to come back, but once he did, that was it. Sasha would talk to him.

The problem was that he still wasn't sure what he was going to tell him.

Knowing Hunter was in danger made Sasha want to say yes. He couldn't deny that, not to himself. But was that a good reason? Or would he say yes just because he was terrified of losing Hunter?

His main worry about bonding with Hunter had been losing him and the pain that would cause. But it looked like he'd feel the same way even though they weren't bonded and they barely knew each other. Hunter had been gone a few days, and Sasha hadn't been able to stop worrying about him. How would bonding with him change that? At least if they were bonded, he'd have an idea about what was happening thanks to the bond. This way, he was obsessing over not having news, and he imagined Hunter dead about every half an hour.

Nate bumped their shoulders together, jerking him out of his thoughts. "You're slacking."

"Sorry."

"Are you okay? Do you need to go home?"

"Nope. I'm fine." Sasha was going to have to tell Nate what was going on sooner or later, but he wasn't sure what was going on himself right now.

Nate didn't look convinced, so Sasha ignored him and went back to work. He managed to serve a few customers before his thoughts went back to Hunter. What was he doing? Would anyone even know to call Sasha to tell him if something happened to him? The only people who knew they were mates were Grey and Nysys, and as far as Sasha knew, they weren't high up in the enforcers' hierarchy. Hell, Nysys probably wasn't even an enforcer, not with all those piercings. It would take him half an hour to take them all out to go on a mission.

Sasha put down a glass of soda on the counter, or at least that was what he thought he was doing, but he missed the counter, and the glass crashed to the floor. Sasha blinked and stared at it.

"That's it," Nate said, pushing Sasha to the side. "Take your break."

Sasha swallowed and crouched to clean the glass and spilled soda. "I'm fine."

"You don't look fine to me, Sasha. I don't know what's going on, but you've broken more glasses today than you have since you started working here. Take your break and try to clear your head, okay?"

Sasha wanted to say no. He wanted to do his job. But he could tell he wasn't working well, and Nate didn't need that, especially not on a Friday night, so he nodded. Nate looked relieved, and a pang of guilt shot through Sasha. Had he really been that bad tonight?

He looked at the broken glass. Yeah, he had. Maybe Nate was right, and he should go home. He didn't think he'd be able to focus on anything today, or even tomorrow. He wouldn't be able to until he knew Hunter was okay.

That gave him his answer, didn't it? No matter how terrified he was of losing Hunter, that wouldn't change if they bonded. He was already in too deep to be able to get out without hurting himself. Besides, he didn't *want* to get out. It had taken him knowing Hunter was in danger to realize that and now he wished Hunter would just come home so they could talk. He still wasn't sure what he wanted, or how fast he wanted it—whatever *it* was—but he was going to give

Hunter a chance.

He finished cleaning up the glass and the soda and went to the break room. He felt like he couldn't breathe, though. The room was too small, and he needed space, away from the worry that weighed on him.

He left the break room and headed outside instead. The parking lot wasn't empty, but the customers were coming and going, and Sasha stuck to the spot that was reserved for the employees. He leaned against the wall by the door and tilted his face toward the dark sky, closing his eyes.

Hunter was in Brazil. What time was it there? *Where* in Brazil was he? Was he safe? Or was he fighting for his life right at that moment? Sasha had no way to know because he couldn't feel what Hunter felt.

He sighed. He wasn't going to solve anything by obsessing over it. The only way he *could* solve this was to wait until Hunter came back and talk to him. And before doing that, he needed to be sure of what he wanted. He wasn't going to force Hunter to wait, not without an explanation. He knew Hunter wouldn't mind waiting if Sasha wanted to take things slow, but Sasha didn't want to make him wait for an answer, not anymore. He hadn't realized how much of a torture it was for him. He wasn't used to caring about someone else anymore. He hadn't thought it would happen again. He hadn't planned to let it happen again. Yet here he was, and he knew he was going to fall in love with Hunter if he let himself do it and get to know him. Not doing that didn't feel like an option anymore.

"Are you okay?"

Sasha opened his eyes to see Grey standing in front of him. He was frowning and leaning close, and Sasha realized he was worried. Really worried, like a friend would be, because even though Sasha had done his best to keep himself isolated when he'd moved to Gillham, he'd made friends anyway. "I'm fine."

Grey nodded and leaned against the wall next to Sasha. "You're worried about Hunter, aren't you?"

"Yes. Have you had any news?"

"No, but that's not surprising. Hunter and I don't belong to the same branch of the enforcers."

"So you wouldn't know if something happened to him."

"I wouldn't be the first to know, but I'd find out eventually. That kind of news has a way of spreading, even to different branches. The fact that I haven't heard anything is good news, Sasha. I promise I'll call you if anything happens, so try not to worry."

"How am I supposed to not do that?"

"I know it's hard. But you're going to have to get used to this if you decide to give Hunter a chance. He's an enforcer, and that's not going to change anytime soon."

Sasha rubbed his face. He'd known that from the start, but that didn't help. How was he supposed to deal with knowing that his mate might be in danger even now?

Hunter stared at the group of men in front of him. Finally, after days of seeing nothing more than trees, trees, and more trees, something was happening.

Michael pressed his body against Hunter's side. "What?" he mouthed.

Hunter tilted his chin toward the people in front of them. He and Michael were hiding in the bushes, and they were ready to grab those guys if Sarah gave them the signal.

Michael nodded and wiggled away. Hunter held his breath, but the three men didn't seem to hear anything. Hunter relaxed. Michael was back within a few minutes, still as silent as he'd been when he'd left. He got on his stomach again and held up three fingers. Hunter frowned and tilted his chin toward the three men. Michael shrugged and held up three fingers again.

Hunter had a hard time believing there were only three men there. The place was being used as a holding area for the drugs that were being made not far away. Their job was to take care of the guys here, and Hunter was pretty sure that putting three men to guard who knew how large a stash of drugs wasn't a smart idea. That didn't mean that wasn't what was happening, because the bad guys were sometimes stupid, but he didn't like this.

There was another team working at the site where the drugs were being made, and they'd raid it at the same time Hunter's team took care of the depot area.

Three men still didn't make sense, though. Even if some of them were ferrying the drugs from the place where they were made, there was a lot of stuff there. Drugs and weapons—nothing anyone would leave laying around without guards.

"Sarah?" he mouthed.

Michael nodded. They waited, both of them staring at the men. And when the signal came, they moved.

Michael took one of the guys while Hunter headed for another. Lucy took the third one.

Hunter knew for sure something was wrong when another two men came crashing from the forest. He swore and dispatched the first guy. The new ones were different, and a sense of dread made his stomach feel like lead.

The first three men had just been guards. *These* men were wearing the Beasts insignia on their jackets. That meant they were shifters, and that they weren't there to play.

Hunter punched the closest guy in the face and stuck his knife into the guys' stomach. He didn't go down, but then, Hunter hadn't expected him to. A good kick in the nuts took care of that, and with the blood dripping from the knife wound, Hunter didn't think he'd have to worry about the guy again.

His heart dropped when he turned and saw that Michael was fighting off two Beasts. He was good, but he was smaller than they were, and even though he managed to avoid several punches and a few of the knife blows, the Beasts finally got to him. The knife pushed into his shoulder, and he screamed. The other Beast took advantage of that and swung his knife, too, digging it into Michael's thigh.

Hunter charged them. He threw the first man to the ground and stuck his knife into his jugular. He didn't wait to make sure the guy was dead. He knew he was, and he didn't have time to waste.

The other Beast was about to slit Michael's throat when Hunter got to him. He hooked his hand under the guys' chin and pulled his head back, sliding his knife along his throat and making sure the cut was deep and long enough that he wouldn't be able to do anything more than gurgling until he died.

Hunter knelt next to Michael. The wounds weren't lethal, but he was losing blood, and he was definitely in pain. "Michael?"

Michael blinked. "That wasn't nice."

Hunter chuckled. "I bet. I'm going to pick you up, okay?"

Michael nodded. Lucy crouched next to Hunter. "Need a hand?"

"No. Go tell Pryderi and Sarah that Michael is wounded, though."

They both got up, and Lucy moved toward the spot where they'd decided to meet once this mess was over. Five guys came crashing out of the forest, right between Lucy and Hunter. Hunter grabbed Michael, hoping he wasn't making the wounds worse by doing so. There was no way he could get through those guys.

He and Lucy looked at each other. He knew she wanted to stay and help, and they might have had a good chance to kill those guys, but it was still five against two, and they also needed to have Michael's back.

There was only one solution. "Go!" he yelled at Lucy.

He turned around and hauled Michael over his shoulder. Then he ran.

He could hear footsteps, people running and screaming behind him, but he didn't turn to look. He knew they were coming after him, and he had to be faster and to find a place to hide. He couldn't fight, not when he had to protect Michael, and the Beasts were a lot more numerous than he was. He'd be killed if he stopped.

Hunter wasn't sure how long he ran before he noticed the cave. It was nothing more than a hole in the ground, but it would be large enough for Michael to hide. "Shift," he told him.

"What about you?"

"Don't worry about that. Come on. I need to keep you safe."

Hunter was relieved when Michael didn't argue. He bundled Michael's clothes and hid them in the bushes before making sure Michael was well hidden. Once he was done, he climbed the closest tree and waited. He'd taken his gun out, but he didn't have an infinite number of bullets.

"Hunter?" Sarah said in his ear.

He swallowed. "Yeah."

"Are you and Michael okay.?"

"For now."

"Pryderi can't shimmer back in."

Hunter bit his lower lip so he wouldn't swear. They'd noticed the machines that were used to keep Nix from shimmering, but they'd been turned off. Now that the Beasts had arrived, Hunter suspected it was because they'd needed to be shimmered in. They'd turned the machines on so Hunter and Michael wouldn't be rescued. He knew Sarah and the rest of the team didn't want to leave, but there was nothing they could do, not on their own. He didn't know exactly how many Beasts were there, but if the five that had come after him and Michael were an indication of anything, they'd need at least two teams, if not three, to take the assholes out.

"We're safe," he murmured.

"We're going back to Whitedell. It's going to take at least a few hours, Hunter. Can Michael make it that long?"

"I think so." He'd have to check the wounds as soon as he was sure the Beasts weren't around anymore, though. All of them had disinfectant and stuff to suture wounds in their cargo pants so that he could help Michael, but that didn't mean he wanted to hang around in the forest. Michael needed a doctor, not Hunter.

"I'll get in touch once we're in Whitedell and we have an idea of what's happening. Those guys came out of nowhere."

"We'll be here." It wasn't like they could leave, not with the Beasts hanging around.

Hunter hoped Michael would still be okay once he thought it was safe for him to climb down the tree and move them to another place. God only knew what could get into his wounds as they waited, and the worst thing that could happen was for him to get his wounds infected. Hunter didn't know how long they were going to have to hang around in the forest, but if the Beasts rallied, it might take a few days for the enforcers to get to them.

He wasn't sure Michael could last that long.

Dammit. Hunter needed to do more, but he didn't know what. The only thing he could do right then was wait and pray the Beasts would get bored of looking for him and Michael and that they'd go back to the place where the drugs and weapons where. The thought of them armed to the teeth wasn't a nice one, but it was better than having them breathing down their necks. Hunter hoped that once he could examine Michael's wounds and tend to them, they'd be able to get out of the Nix shield and get Pryderi to pick them up.

He didn't really believe that, though.

Sasha was glad the day was over and that the bar was empty. He'd volunteered to do most of the clean-up so Nate wouldn't have to do both his job and Sasha's. He'd taken on most of the bartending that night because of how distracted Sasha had been, so it was the least Sasha could do. He didn't mind going to bed a bit later than usual. He'd have plenty of time to sleep anyway.

He put more glasses in the dishwasher and closed it, turning it on. He still needed to mop the floors, but then he'd go home. Nate had already gone upstairs since Sasha had his own key.

The door banged open. Sasha yelped and turned around, holding his broom up as a weapon. It wouldn't do much, but it would be better than going down without fighting.

Nysys strode in. Sasha's heart was still racing, but he put down the broom and sighed. "You couldn't shimmer in? You didn't use the door last time." He smiled, hoping Nysys would understand he was teasing. He was, even though he wished Nysys wouldn't scare the crap out of him every time he wanted to talk.

Nysys wasn't smiling.

Sasha cleared his throat. "Don't take that badly."

"I'm not. Sasha, we need to talk."

"Now? Because I was just closing. I need to go to bed."

"Something's happened."

Sasha froze. "Something's happened? What do you

mean?"

"To Hunter."

Sasha needed to sit down. He used the broom to keep himself up. He was petrified. He didn't want to ask Nysys what had happened or if Hunter was hurt, or worse, dead. He didn't want certainty. He wasn't sure he could take it. "How bad is it?" he forced himself to ask.

"We're not sure. Come on. I came to get you so we can go back to Whitedell."

"What?"

"To talk to Hunter's team and Dominic. They're all meeting right now to try to find a way to get Hunter and Michael back."

So Hunter wasn't dead. That helped Sasha breathe more easily, but the knot of worry and dread was still firmly placed in his stomach, and he wasn't sure it was going to leave until Hunter was in front of him, safe and sound. "Is he..."

"He's okay from what I know. But one of his friends and team members is wounded. That's why Hunter stayed. To help Michael. He's protecting him. But you'll get more answers once we're at the mansion."

"Give me a minute." Sasha wanted to go right away, but Nate would freak out of he didn't come into work tomorrow, especially since it was a Saturday, so Sasha quickly climbed the stairs to tell him what was happening.

"I'm coming with you," Nate said as soon as he heard.

"No. I don't know what's going on exactly, and I've never been to Whitedell. I don't know how they're going to take my presence there. I doubt most of them know I'm Hunter's mate."

Nate scowled. "You hadn't even told me."

"I'm sorry. I was just trying to figure things out." A wave of affection made Sasha kiss Nate's cheek. "Thank you. I'll call you as soon as I know something."

"I'll be waiting. And don't try to rush back here. Take all the time you need. I don't want to see you again unless your mate is with you."

Sasha was relieved Nate didn't mind. He was a good boss, and even though Sasha hadn't realized it, a friend.

Nysys was waiting in the bar when Sasha got back. He was tapping his foot with his arms crossed over his chest. He nodded when Sasha got back and held his hand out. Sasha had never shimmered. He'd made a point of avoiding anything weird or magical since Cedric's death. He had to get over that now, though. He didn't have the time to drive to Whitedell.

He took Nysys' hand and closed his eyes.

The sudden sound of voices made him open them. He was now in a large office full of people. They were talking over each other, pointing at a map. Nysys cleared his throat, and when no one noticed him, he yelled. "People!"

Everyone shut up and turned around. One of the men sighed and pinched the bridge of his nose. "Nysys. What are you doing here?"

"I brought someone."

"Now's not the moment. We have to deal with this before something happens to Hunter and Michael. Take your friend and go."

"He's not just my friend."

"Nysys—"

"This is Sasha, Hunter's mate. And we're both staying."

There was a moment of silence during which *everyone* stared at Sasha. He pulled his hair In front of his face and prayed they'd stop. God, he hated it when people stared at him.

The man cleared his throat. "I didn't know Hunter had found his mate."

Nysys arched a brow. "You would if you'd bothered asking me instead of shooing me out like a kid. But don't worry. I don't hold grudges."

The man snorted. "Sure you don't." He came closer and offered Sasha his hand. "I'm Dominic."

Sasha swallowed. "Dominic Nash?"

Dominic smiled. "Yes. And you're welcome to this meeting, of course. As Hunter's mate, you have the right to know what's happening."

Nysys looped his arm around Sasha's. "And since he's going to tell me everything anyway, I might as well stay."

Dominic sighed. "As long as you don't stick your nose into this. I know you mean well, but this isn't your job, and we have to be quick."

Nysys made the gesture of zipping his lips shut. Dominic rolled his eyes, but it seemed to be enough for him. He gestured toward the table. "Come. This is Nate, my beta, and Sarah, Hunter's team leader. We're expecting the local head of the enforcers soon."

"What happened?" No one had yet told Sasha that, and he wanted to know.

"Hunter stayed behind to save Michael," Sarah said. "Michael is wounded. He was stabbed twice. I managed to talk to Hunter before the communications were cut off, and he's okay. He's not wounded, and for now, he's safe."

Sasha collapsed into one of the empty chairs, his knees weak with relief. "Not wounded?"

"No. Lucy, one of the other team members, was there with them. She managed to get back to me, and she told me what happened. Hunter confirmed he was okay."

"What happens now? Why can't you send a Nix to get them?"

Sarah shook her head. "The . . . people who attacked us were prepared. They not only cut our communications, but they also put a Nix shield into place. That means no Nix can go in or come out. We're going to have to go on foot, but there are a lot of people there now, so we need to put together several teams. An alternative would be for Hunter and Michael to come to us, but the Beasts are no doubt prepared for that to happen. I wouldn't be surprised if they're still looking for them. They're moving the drugs and the weapons they still have on site, but they won't want anyone putting their business at risk."

The Beasts. Sasha had heard about the gang, just like everyone else. They thought humans weren't good enough to clean their boots. They were drug dealers and had their hands in weapon trafficking and prostitution. They were killers.

And Hunter was right in the middle of a big group of them.

Sasha buried his face in his hands. He couldn't believe how much he'd messed up. He'd know what Hunter was feeling right now if he'd agreed to bond with him. He might have been able to help.

And even worse, if something happened to Hunter and he died, he'd never know that Sasha wanted him.

"Are you okay?" Dominic asked.

Sasha nodded even though he wasn't sure he was.

Sarah cleared her throat. "It would help us if you could tell us how Hunter is feeling right now."

"I don't know. We haven't bonded. We just met. He was giving me time to get used to the idea."

Her expression fell. "Of course. I understand. Well it was worth a try, but don't worry, we'll get Hunter and Michael back. This is what we do. We have protocols in place for this kind of situation, so we know Hunter is going to try to find a place where he and Michael can hide out until we manage to get to them."

"How long is that going to take?"

Sarah and Dominic looked at each other. She licked her lips. "We don't know yet, but we're doing the best we can."

But would it be enough?

Hunter wasn't sure how much time had passed, but he knew he and Michael wouldn't be discovered. The Beasts had passed under his tree a few times, but they hadn't found either of them. He'd waited a while after their last passage, but he couldn't wait any longer. He needed to tend to Michael before his wounds got infected.

He waited for another heartbeat, then he put his gun away and slithered down the tree. He wished he could shift into his python form—it would be safer, even though the Beasts were shifters, too, and would be able to scent he wasn't a real animal—but he needed his hands.

"Michael?" he called, his voice barely more than a murmur.

Something rustled in the bushes. Michael's head poked out of the hole that Hunter had stuck him into earlier, and Hunter breathed easier. Michael was moving, so that was good. He didn't seem to be in too much pain when Hunter got close to the hole, and he tried to climb out. Hunter helped him, and once he'd shifted back to his human form, he helped him put on the t-shirt he'd taken off earlier. "How are you feeling?"

Michael glared. "Like someone stabbed me a few times."

"Right. Okay, hold still. I'm going to clean the wounds and stitch them. I'll try to be as fast and careful as I can, but I'm not Pryderi."

"Unfortunately."

Hunter didn't take offense. He wouldn't have wanted to be stitched either, not when they were used to being healed by Pryderi when they got hurt. Nix healing had spoiled them, and now Michael would get to see exactly how much.

Hunter took out what he'd need from his pockets. It wouldn't be the same as being in a hospital, but he'd do his best. "They'll probably scar. Sorry. But hey, you'll look more rugged. That'll attract the guys."

Michael's glare deepened. Hunter decided it would be better for him to keep his mouth shut, at least until he was done taking care of Michael. He rather liked his teeth where they were, and Michael looked ready to knock them out.

The wounds were deep, especially the one on Michael's thigh. It made Hunter's stomach churn, something he wasn't sure how to explain. He was used to blood and gore. They were part of his job. But usually, the blood and gore came from people he didn't care about, not from his friends. Even when someone on the team had been wounded in the past, Pryderi had been there to start healing them before taking them back to the enforcers' house. Now, though, Hunter was the only one Michael could rely on, and he was far from being a healer.

He cleaned the wounds as much as he could, trying to get all the blood and dirt from the forest out of it. Michael didn't say a word, but he hissed a few times, and his jaw was so tense that it looked like it might break.

The process was lengthy even though Hunter tried to hurry. Michael relaxed once Hunter was done, and he let Hunter bandage the wounds after he'd stitched them without protesting. Hunter could see he was in pain, though. He was pale and looked like he could sleep for a week. His skin was damp with sweat, although that could be from the hot as hell temperature. They were in a fucking jungle after all.

Hunter patted Michael's leg. "All done."

Michael relaxed and leaned more heavily against the trunk behind his back. "What now?"

Hunter looked around. He knew what he would have done if he'd been alone, but he wasn't, and Michael wasn't in good enough shape to walk toward a zone that wouldn't be shielded from Nix. "I talked with Sarah earlier, when I was in the tree."

"What did she say?"

"That for the moment, we're stuck here. They're going to come back, but now that they know we're here, the Beasts have called more men, and there's no way one team of enforcers can make it through to us." Hunter didn't like the thought of sticking around and waiting, though. He could see Michael needed a healer, and the sooner, the better. With so many Beasts in the area, it would take a while to coordinate enough enforcers and take over, and he wasn't sure Michael could wait that long. He didn't want to find out what would happen if he had to.

What alternative did he have, though?

Hunter dug a few protein bars from Michael's pockets and handed them to him. "Eat. You'll need to shift back once you're done. I have to check the perimeter. With you hurt, we need to be sure the area is relatively safe. I'm going to have to sleep soon." Hunter hoped that the fact that it was night would keep the Beasts to their tents or whatever the hell they used, but he wouldn't swear on that. They were shifters, and some of their animals wouldn't have a problem seeing in the dark.

No, they couldn't risk it. They couldn't stay around and wait for someone to save them. It was too dangerous.

Hunter was going to have to do the saving.

That was fine. It was his job, and he knew how to do it. Hell, it was the one thing he was actually good at.

Michael shifted after eating. He looked tired, and Hunter made sure he was well hidden before leaving. He hoped Michael would be able to sleep some because he wanted them to move as soon as he came back.

There were Beasts all over the forest. Most of them had gathered where the weapons and drugs were, and they were moving them to trucks. At least that meant they were distracted from looking for Hunter and Michael. Hunter managed to find out where the Nix shield ended, and he was pretty sure he could walk there with Michael in his arms. Michael was light when he was in his fox form. What worried Hunter was that if his arms were busy, he wouldn't be able to defend them if they were attacked. Still, it was worth a try, but not tonight. He wanted to explore the forest more in the daylight, and Michael needed to sleep and eat some more. Hopefully, Hunter had done a good job on his wounds and the antibiotics he'd give him once he was back would help keep infections away.

Hunter managed to avoid the Beasts as he went back to Michael, but it was a close thing. He was lucky the ones he almost stumbled onto were too busy fucking to notice him. He was tempted to kill them because it would mean he and Michael would have fewer people after them, but two men wouldn't make a difference, and he didn't want to draw attention to the part of the forest where Michael was currently hiding.

Michael was asleep when Hunter got back to his hiding place. He was tempted to grab the fox and make a run for it, but now wasn't the time. He needed to contact Sarah and tell her what he was going to do, check with her whether there was any way she could send someone to help. She probably wouldn't, because it would be too dangerous, and in the end, the main objective of their mission had been to grab the drugs and as many of the people working there and stick their asses in jail. That didn't mean they weren't going to try to help Michael and Hunter, but they were only two, while taking the drugs and neutralizing the Beasts would help hundreds of people. Sarah and the rest of the team wouldn't be happy, but they didn't make the decisions. The council did.

Hunter knelt next to Michael's hidey-hole and gently touched the top of his head. It took him a while to coax Michael into a state that was awake enough that he shifted. Hunter barely managed to keep the swearing in when he realized Michael was starting to get too warm. It might just be the temperature in the jungle, but he doubted it. He gave Michael the antibiotics and checked his wounds. They still looked good, or as good as they could anyway, but he didn't think that was going to last much longer. No, he was going to have to get Michael out of there tomorrow.

They just needed to walk far enough that they could leave the Nix shield. Then Pryderi would come get them, and Michael would be safe.

Maybe if Hunter repeated that to himself enough times, he'd start to believe it.

Chapter Five

Sasha wanted to punch something—or someone—he wouldn't be particular about it. If he was honest, he kind of wanted to use Dominic as a punching bag, even though the man had let him stay in for the meeting. The problem was that even though this meeting had lasted for hours before Dominic had sent everyone to bed, it hadn't solved anything.

"You need to relax," Nysys said, leaning against Sasha's side.

Sasha snorted. "Relax? Are you seriously telling me that?"

"I know it's not easy. Trust me, I didn't want to go to bed either, and neither did Hunter and Michael's team. But Dominic was right. We'd all been going on fumes, and we won't be able to help Hunter and Michael that way."

Sasha couldn't deny that, but it wasn't like he'd slept. He'd been given a guest room, and he'd spent a few hours flopping around in bed and waiting until it was late enough to go back to the office. It was barely six in the morning, but he and Nysys were there, as was Sarah. Dominic was taking longer, but Nysys had told Sasha he had a mate and children, so Sasha was doing his best not to be pissed.

It wasn't working. "We need to get to Hunter as soon as possible. Isn't that what they said last night? That Michael is wounded and that he needs to be healed? Why are we still here, then?"

"Well, *you* are here because you're human and I'm not going to let you go anywhere near that jungle," Dominic said as he walked in, the shoulder of his shirt obviously wet.

"I know I'm only human," Sasha said. The words felt like ash in his mouth, but he couldn't say anything else. He couldn't reveal his secret, not when he didn't know the people in the room with him. He couldn't tell how they'd react, and he needed them right now because he was *not* going to lose someone else.

He hadn't realized how much he needed Hunter in his life until he was losing him, and he hated that. He wouldn't forbid Hunter from being an enforcer, but as much as it scared him, he'd decided he still wanted him. He didn't know what was going to happen, if or when he was going to lose him, or even if he would be able to open up to someone else, but he was going to try—as soon as he got Hunter back. Hunter had said they could go slow, and Sasha was probably going to need that, but he was done staying away and hoping Hunter forgot about him because now that he knew what *that* was like, he realized how bad it made him feel.

"We need to wait. There's no way we can take that number of Beasts on," Dominic said, jerking Sasha out of his thoughts.

He blinked. What had he missed? "What?"

Dominic didn't say anything about how distracted Sasha was. "Sarah just told me that more Beasts arrived during the night. They're moving the weapons and the drugs, and they'll stick around until everything is out. We could go in, but we'd stand to lose several enforcers."

"This way you stand to lose Hunter and Michael," Sasha said between gritted teeth.

Dominic rubbed his face. "I know. I realize that, and I don't like it. I hope the Beasts will leave them be and that we'll be able to go in to get them, but we have to wait. This wouldn't be a problem if they didn't have the Nix shield in place, but they do, so the only way in for us is straightforward, and there are too many men there right now. I don't want this to escalate into a war."

"But—"

"We're going to do everything we can, but this is it right now. Hunter isn't wounded, so unless he does something stupid, he'll be fine."

"What about Michael?" Now that Nysys had told him who Michael was, Sasha remembered seeing him at the bar a few times. He looked sweet, and Hunter genuinely liked him from what Sasha had observed. He didn't want anyone to die, not when there had to be a way to help. It didn't matter that Michael wasn't Sasha's mate or that they didn't even know each other.

"You *have* to do something."

"I want to, but right now, it's out of the question. We're monitoring the number of Beasts in the forest, and we'll go in as soon as they get manageable. But right now, they're crawling everywhere, and I will *not* lose my enforcers in what is clearly a desperate mission we can't bring to term. I hate this as much as you do, trust me. I don't want to lose anyone, and I like Hunter and Michael. I consider them friends. They're not the only ones, though, and as a council member, I have to consider what's best for everyone, not just for them." He sighed heavily. "You can stay here until we know more, of course. I'm sure Nysys can get you back home to Gillham so you can grab some clothes. The guest room will be yours until Hunter and Michael are back."

The conversation was over. Sarah looked like she wanted to protest, too, but she didn't. She pressed her lips together and nodded at Sasha.

He wanted to stay. He wanted to tell Dominic to send someone, *anyone*, and get Hunter and Michael home. He could tell he wouldn't change the alpha's mind, though, and he realized the man wasn't wrong. *He* didn't care about anyone but Hunter, though.

He stomped out of the room and headed in the general direction of the guest room where he'd spent the night. He was already thinking about what he could do to help, though.

He stopped and looked at his hands. Could whatever had been done to him be used for good? He'd never thought that, but then, he tried not to think about anything that happened in the lab or that was related to his power. It had hurt him too much.

"Come on. I'll shimmer you home," Nysys said, gently pushing Sasha.

Sasha turned to look at him. They were alone in the hallway, and he hoped that was how things would stay. "You can shimmer."

Nysys arched a brow. "I know that. You do, too. Is the stress getting to you?"

Sasha shook his head. "What I meant is that you can shimmer me to Hunter."

Nysys' eyes widened. "Oh, no. Nope. I'm not doing that."

"Why not?"

"*Why not?* Why do you think, Sasha? How about because you're human and the Beasts would tear you apart? Or maybe because Dominic told us to stay here? Or, wait, because *I* don't want to die?"

"I need to get there. Please. Wouldn't you go if your mate was the one stuck in that jungle?"

Nysys glared. "You know I would."

"Then you understand why I have to go."

"I also understand you're human, Sasha, and while I'm a Nix, I can't fight. Once we're there—*if* we go—what are we going to do? You heard Dom. The place is full of Beasts, and those guys make Satan look like a nice guy. We're going to get killed before we even manage to find Hunter and

Michael."

Sasha bit his lower lip. He *really* didn't want to do this. He'd avoided it for as long as he could. But what if this was the only way to get to Hunter before it was too late? "I was captured by the Glass Research Company," he said, wishing he didn't have to.

Nysys blinked. "You were?"

"Yes."

"Oh, poor you. Are you one of the people who accepted Morin's money when he sold the company?"

Sasha frowned. "What?"

"My mate, Morin. You know he's the son of the man who did all that horrible stuff, right?"

"How am I supposed to know that if you didn't tell me?" And while Sasha did want to talk about that, they didn't have the time, not right now. "Anyway, I'm still human, but the experiments they did on me changed me. I have... powers."

Nysys cocked his head. "What kind of power?"

"I can make people and things explode."

"Really?"

"Yes." He didn't tell Nysys that he couldn't control that power, though. He needed to go to that jungle, and he needed to do it now. "Please. I can take care of the Beasts."

Nysys still looked like he wanted to say no, and Sasha could have kissed him when he nodded. "All right. I don't want Hunter and Michael to get hurt any more than you do. Come on. We need uniforms."

Hunter held Michael close to his chest and peeked around the tree. He'd heard voices, and he fucking hoped the Beasts weren't still looking for them.

They'd had to move twice during the night, and Hunter

had made sure they went toward the Nix shield's edge rather than deeper in the jungle. It was a risk, but he hoped they'd be able to cross the shield. He had no doubt Pryderi was looking for them, and he'd find them as soon as they crossed.

They had to get there first, though.

Michael was still in bad shape, so Hunter had him shift. It was easier to carry him in his fox form, although Hunter wished he could read Michael's fox expression better. He could only tell Michael was in pain, but that was all, and he already knew that.

He stroked the top of Michael's head. "You doing okay, buddy?" he murmured.

Michael scowled at him. Hunter prayed that meant he was well enough considering the situation, but he didn't have time to make sure. The voices were coming closer.

"I'm going to have to put you down," he told Michael.

Michael nodded.

Hunter made sure he was hidden by leaves and whatever he could find on the ground. It wasn't great, but it would take anyone a second look to see him, which was better than Hunter had hoped to manage.

He turned his focus on the people coming. They were trying to be discreet, but they weren't succeeding. Hunter rolled his eyes when one of them tripped and swore so loud even people in the next country had to have heard him. If this was the kind of people the Beasts recruited, then they'd end up destroying themselves without needing any help from the enforcers.

He waited until they were close enough to jump away from the tree and grab the first guy. He squeaked and tried to wiggle out of Hunter's arm while the other guy hit Hunter's back while yelling, "Let him go!"

Hunter obeyed, too stunned to do anything else. He

looked down at Sasha, who'd ended up in his arms. "What the fuck?"

"Oh, thank God. I thought we were going to have to walk for *hours* to find you," Nysys complained. "I already have blisters. How can you stand walking around in these boots? I want to tear them off and burn them."

"What the fuck?" Hunter repeated.

Sasha grabbed his arms. "Where's Michael?"

"Behind that tree."

"Good. Take him. We have to go before the Beasts realize we're here. Come on."

Hunter had so many questions, but he realized he didn't have the time to ask them, not right now. As soon as they were back in Whitedell, though, he *was* going to ask them, and to demand answers.

He brushed the leaves out of Michael's fur and hauled him into his arms again. Michael stuck his nose against Hunter's neck, and Hunter patted his back. "You'll be fine. Help is here." Now they just had to get out of the shield.

Hunter handed Michael to Nysys. "Carry him."

Nysys wrinkled his nose. "No offense, but he's dirty."

"That's because we just spent a week in the jungle. Come on. I need to be able to fight if I have to, and neither you nor Sasha are up to that."

"But Sasha has his superpowers," Nysys said, wiggling his fingers.

Hunter frowned and added that to the list of questions he had, especially because Sasha looked like he would do just about anything to avoid answering it. "Where are the others?"

Nysys was suddenly interested in Michael. He petted his fur and murmured to him, leading the way toward the shield and leaving Hunter and Sasha behind.

"Sasha?" Hunter asked. He needed to have at least an

idea of what was going on.

Sasha sighed. "There's only us."

"What do you mean?"

"Dominic said we'd have to wait to send someone to get you because there are so many Beasts in the jungle, so no one else is coming."

"Are you crazy? You and Nysys came here on your *own*?"

Sasha raised his chin and looked at Hunter. "Yeah, we did. Because no one else was going to and we didn't want to lose you or Michael. Now shut up and let's go." He grabbed Hunter's hand and pulled, and he didn't let go, not even when Hunter obeyed.

Hunter wasn't sure how to deal with this new, forceful Sasha. He wasn't sure of anything right now, actually. He'd thought Sasha wouldn't even notice he was gone, or if he had, that he'd be glad for the reprieve. How had he ended up in the Brazilian rainforest?

"What are you doing here?" he asked.

"I thought we were going to talk about this later?"

"Come on, Sasha. You know why I'm asking. Why are you here?"

Sasha didn't look at Hunter. "Because no one else was going to come, not right now. I didn't want to risk you or Michael getting hurt or dying."

"You're not a fighter."

"I'm not."

"Neither is Nysys."

"Are we talking about what's obvious?" Nysys asked. "I want to play, too. Let's see. The sky is blue. The forest is fucking damp and too hot. Hunter is an idiot."

Hunter wasn't even angry at Nysys' insult. He was glad to see him and Sasha and worried as hell because he knew all too well what would happen to them if the Beasts found them. It was a miracle that they'd managed to sneak into the forest considering how loud they were, especially Nysys, who didn't seem to understand that this was supposed to be a covert mission and that it wouldn't end well for any of them if the Beasts noticed them.

"Keep your voice down," he told Nysys.

Nysys turned and glared at him. "So ungrateful. We came here to save your hairy ass when no one else was going to, and this is how you thank us?"

"I'll thank you any way you want me to once we're home, but we'll never get there if the Beasts hear us and decide to kill us."

Nysys waved. "Sasha will just blow them to bits."

Sasha grimaced. "About that—"

Something crashed out of the forest, hitting Hunter on the side. The air whooshed out of his lungs, and he slammed against a tree, the bark shredding the skin on his cheek. He didn't focus on the pain, though. He grabbed the man who'd hit him, wrapping his arm around his neck, and punched him on the nose. The man howled and moved back, giving Hunter enough time to take his gun out and shoot him between the eyes.

The Beast hadn't been alone.

When Hunter turned, he saw Nysys, his back against a tree, his eyes wide as he watched Sasha fight with a second man. Sasha was losing. He wasn't a fighter, and the Beast seemed to know that because the asshole was grinning as he easily avoided Sasha's small fists.

Hunter could hear other people coming, so he ran to Nysys and shook him. "Go!"

Nysys shook his head. "I can't leave you and Sasha."

"Yes, you can. I'll take care of him. You know that. Take Michael home and make sure he's healed. Tell Dominic and Sarah what happened. They'll know what to do."

"But—"

"Go, Nysys, before they kill you and Michael."

Nysys finally moved. They weren't far from the Nix shield, and Hunter looked at him until he shimmered away.

Then he turned on the man beating his mate up.

He didn't want to waste a bullet, but this would be the best and fastest way to kill the guy, grab Sasha, and run away before the other Beasts arrived. There was no way Hunter and Sasha could take care of them if there were too many, and Hunter's main objective right now was to keep his mate safe. Sasha already had a bloody nose and lip, and that was too much for Hunter's taste.

He waited until the Beast's back was to him to yell, "Sasha, down!" he prayed Sasha would obey because he didn't want to risk his mate being wounded by the bullet if it went through.

He fired. The bullet hit the Beast on the upper left side of the back. He went down like a potato sack, and he didn't try to get up, so Hunter was pretty sure he was dead.

He didn't stick around to check.

He grabbed Sasha's hand and pulled like Sasha had done with him earlier.

Sasha trusted Hunter to know where he was going, or at the very least, to be able to avoid slamming both of them into a tree as they ran. Everything looked the same to Sasha—trees everywhere. He couldn't even see the sky because of them.

He could hear people yelling behind them, and he hoped they weren't following. They'd left before those other men could get to them, so maybe they didn't know which way they'd gone.

Sasha didn't really believe that. Those people were shifters. They could probably smell his fear from where they were. They'd only have to follow that to find him and

Hunter. What the fuck had he been thinking when he'd decided to come? He'd wanted to save Hunter and Michael, and he supposed he had succeeded, at least in part. Michael was no doubt being healed right now.

But now *Sasha* was in trouble.

Hunter stopped suddenly, and Sasha almost hit his back. "What?"

Hunter patted his pockets down and took out a small white bottle with a spray on top. Sasha's eyes widened when he sprayed first himself, then Sasha, before putting the spray back and pulling Sasha into a run again. "What did you do?" Sasha asked before he had to focus all his breathing on running.

"Hid our scents!"

That was good. Now the only thing the Beasts would be able to follow was Sasha's heavy breathing. He might even have a heart attack and drop dead before they got to him. He certainly felt like he was about to.

He didn't know how long they ran, but it was way past when they stopped hearing anything that wasn't made by animals.

Hunter finally stopped, and Sasha flopped on the ground. He didn't even care that it was damp. He was sweating anyway, so much that he might as well have taken a bath. He sucked in a breath and closed his eyes, leaning back against the closest tree and praying he wasn't about to die.

"Are you okay?"

Sasha opened his eyes. Hunter was crouching in front of him, and he was barely panting, the asshole. "I'll live."

Hunter grinned, but there was no humor in his smile. "Good, because I want to kill you myself for being so stupid that you came here, and with Nysys of all people. How do you even know him?"

"He came to talk to me after we met. He wanted me to

give you a chance."

Hunter shook his head. "Of course he did. He always sticks his nose into everything. But you shouldn't have come, Sasha."

"Probably not. I still don't regret it."

"That's because you're an idiot."

"An idiot who saved Michael's life." Sasha didn't care that Hunter was angry, but he could do without the insults.

Hunter rubbed his face. "I know. Sorry. But do you know how terrified I was when you took on that guy? He would have killed you if I hadn't shot him."

"But you stopped him."

"Thank fuck I did." He held a hand out. "Now come on. We're far enough away that I don't think they're going to find us, but we should find a place where we can spend the night. It can get cold, and I want to be secure enough that we can both sleep, because I won't be able to do much tomorrow otherwise. It's probably going to take us a while to find a suitable spot."

Sasha knew Hunter was right, even though he felt like he was going to die if he took one more step. He didn't have an alternative, though. Hunter wouldn't leave him behind if he wasn't up to walking, but then they'd both be vulnerable.

So Sasha walked. He couldn't remember the last time he'd walked this much. He was out of practice, because he hadn't gone hiking since Cedric's death.

He followed Hunter, who was strangely silent. He never was. Sasha knew that because of the many times he'd watched him. He knew Hunter was angry. He understood it. He was still happy he'd come, though. Even if he never got out of this damn jungle, he and Nysys had gotten Michael to safety. Of course, that meant that Sasha was now going to have to spend time with Hunter, but wasn't that what he'd wanted before?

Okay, so he'd panicked when Dominic had said he wasn't sending anyone. Sasha should have thought this through instead of lying to Nysys to convince him to take him here. But he still couldn't think about another option, not even now that he was in the middle of a jungle. And even if Hunter couldn't forgive him, he wouldn't regret it. He might have wasted his chance with his . . . mate, but he'd saved a life.

Sasha's legs felt like lead, but he pushed on. He pushed through Hunter's silence, through the warm, sticky heat, through the insects that were eating him alive, through the exhaustion because he hadn't slept the night before.

His foot caught in a dead branch, and he stumbled. He tried to keep himself upright, but he was already tilting, and he knew his face was going to take the brunt of it if he didn't put his hands forward.

Strong hands grabbed his arm and kept him upright. He leaned against Hunter's side and was surprised when Hunter didn't push him away. Instead, he briefly hugged Sasha once he was steadier on his feet and asked, "You okay?"

"Just tired."

"God, me too. Want to tell me what happened so I can think about something that's not my bed?"

Sasha chuckled. He *didn't* want to talk about it, but he felt he owed Hunter at least that. "I told you, Dominic wasn't going to send anyone yet, and I know how much you care for Michael."

They started walking again. Hunter was silent, but Sasha could feel him looking at him.

"What?" he asked.

"I get that, and while I'm angry, I know Michael wouldn't be back home right now if you and Nysys hadn't come. So thank you. What I *don't* get is *why* you're here. I haven't seen you or heard from you since we talked in the park. I thought that was all the answer I needed, but it looks like I might have been wrong."

"I . . . panicked." Sasha might as well be honest.

"How did you even find out I was missing?"

"Nysys came to me. He'd already been to the bar to tell me about you, how I needed to give you a chance and that I could at least text you or something. He and Grey got me thinking. Well, them, and the fact that I was worried about you. I didn't think I would be, but then Nysys told me you were missing, and I just had to do something."

"And that something was letting Nysys drag you here?"

"He didn't drag me. He didn't even want to come. I had to lie to him to convince him to bring me here."

"About that power of yours?"

"In part. Can we talk about this later? I *really* have to sit down, and maybe drink."

"Did you bring supplies?"

"No. I didn't think much beyond having to get here to save you." Sasha expected Hunter to sneer at that, but he smiled instead. "Why are you smiling?" He had to know.

"Because you were so scared for me that you rushed here without thinking."

"And that's something to smile about?"

"It is, at least for me. It means you care."

"Of course I do."

"Well, excuse me if I wasn't sure. You haven't exactly been forthcoming with what you feel toward me."

And once again, Hunter was right. "I'm sorry."

"Don't worry about it. Why don't you sit down? I think we're far enough away that the Beasts won't find us here, and you can rest while I look for a place to spend the night. There are caves around here. I can probably find one that's not too big, and that's empty of animals."

Sasha looked around. "I'm not sure I want to be alone."

"Don't worry. I won't go far. Just scream if you're attacked, and I'll be right back. But I doubt anyone will find you."

"Why not?"

"Because of the spray. It canceled your scent. That way the Beasts can't find us, and neither can wild animals."

Sasha supposed that should make him feel better.

It didn't.

Hunter couldn't help thinking about what Sasha had done. He was pissed, but that was mostly because he was terrified. Sasha could have been hurt, or worse. And what if Hunter hadn't already been on his way toward the Nix shield? Sasha and Nysys would have been taken by the Beasts, and Hunter didn't even want to think about what would have been done to them. At best, they would have been used for ransom or to bargain with the council.

Sasha wasn't wrong, though. If he and Nysys hadn't come, Michael would have no doubt gotten worse, and Hunter couldn't think about that, either. Michael was his best friend on the team and one of his best friends in the world. He didn't know what he'd do if he lost him, and he would have been angry with the council for not helping, even though he understood why they were waiting. He prayed they wouldn't wait too long, though. He didn't like the thought of Sasha being in danger, and that was right smack where he was right now.

Hunter tried not to think too much about that as he looked for a cave. He knew for a fact there were several of them around. He just needed to find one that wasn't too big or inhabited by wild animals.

The one he found was partially hidden by trees and low hanging lianas. The floor was damp at the entrance, but it dried out further in the cave. It was deep, too deep for Hunter to explore it, but it would do. Hopefully, nothing would attack them from behind. It was enough for them not to have to worry about the Beasts finding them.

Hunter went back to get Sasha. He smiled when he realized Sasha was sleeping, his back still against the tree, his head lolling forward. He wasn't used to this, to walking so much and running, or fearing for his life. Hunter still couldn't believe he was there, that he'd come for him, especially after the way he'd ignored him for days. It gave him hope, and he definitely wanted to talk about it, but first, he needed to get Sasha to the cave and get some food into him. He still had a few protein bars, so dinner was set.

Hunter crouched next to Sasha and gently touched his shoulder. "Sasha?"

Sasha jerked awake, his eyes wide, his head snapping left and right as he looked for the threat. Hunter raised his hands so Sasha could see he wasn't going to hurt him. Sasha blinked. "What?"

"You fell asleep. Come on. I found a cave. We can spend the night there."

Sasha nodded. He looked exhausted, and Hunter considered carrying him to the cave so he could sleep. He knew it was impossible, though. The terrain was rough, and he'd already had a hard time with Michael, who'd been in his fox form. A full-grown man would throw both of them to the ground, and they needed to avoid injuries.

Sasha followed Hunter in silence. The only sound they made was their footsteps, and it mingled with the sound of the forest. Hunter doubted the Beasts would find them here. They were trying to get their things out of the jungle as soon as possible. They knew the council was gunning for them, and that the only reason they hadn't come back yet was that there were too many Beasts around. That was why they'd called so many members.

They clambered down into the cave and Sasha looked around, his hands on his hips. "This is it?"

Hunter grinned. "I'm sorry it lacks comfort, but you know how it is. The comfier caves were already taken. You should have booked sooner."

Sasha rolled his eyes. "Okay, okay. I won't bore you with my complaints. I'm just not used to this anymore. It's been a while since I last went camping and hiking." His voice had a hint of sadness, and Hunter wanted to know more about that. He wanted to ask Sasha questions and listen to his answers. He knew he wouldn't get anything, not this early in their relationship, but he felt like they'd already made such huge steps forward just by Sasha coming to get him and being worried about him enough to do something that dangerous and crazy.

But first, they needed to settle down for the night. It was going to be dark, and they couldn't light a fire because Hunter didn't want the Beasts to notice them. That meant they had to make sure they were as comfortable as possible in the few hours of light they had left.

He sent Sasha out to gather supplies with the promise Sasha wouldn't stray too far away. Once he was back, Hunter left. He knew what he was looking for. It wasn't the first night he'd had to spend in the jungle, and while he wished he still had his sleeping bag, he could build something that would help keep him and Sasha dry and as warm as possible. They might have to sleep pressed together, but Hunter wasn't going to complain about that.

Together, they managed to build a small platform that would keep the chill of the ground and most animals away. They used palm fronds to make a low ceiling and isolate the sides. Hunter could have done a better job, but considering how little time he'd had, he was satisfied.

He and Sasha settled into their little hut. Sasha kept some distance between them, and Hunter hoped he would come closer later in the night. It was almost completely dark by now, and Sasha was human. He didn't have the better eyesight Hunter had, and he'd be confused if he fell off the platform in the middle of the night while he was sleeping.

"Is the room to your taste?" Hunter teased.

Sasha chuckled. "It's better than what I thought."

"Yeah?"

"We're not sleeping on the ground, so that's good."

"It is. Can I offer you a prime protein bar? There's peanut butter in them."

"I love peanut butter."

Hunter knew it was ridiculous, but his chest puffed out at the pleasure of making his mate happy. He hadn't let himself think that way before because he hadn't been sure Sasha would even want to talk to him again, let alone want to bond with him eventually. He thought he had a better chance now, though, so he let himself hope.

Sasha started moving closer once the night set in and the sky was entirely dark. Hunter didn't say anything about it. He stayed still and let Sasha settle down the way he wanted to and was most comfortable.

Then he pounced, because he fucking wanted answers. "What did you mean when you said you didn't quite lie to Nysys about that power he thinks you have."

Sasha's body went rigid for a moment, but then he huffed and relaxed. "I'd hoped you forgot about that."

Hunter snorted. "Fat chance of that."

"God, I don't want to talk about this."

Hunter frowned. "You don't actually have to. I mean, I'd like it if you trusted me enough to tell me, and if you felt comfortable enough with me, but I'm not going to push you, or, I don't know, to pout or whatever if you don't. I already told you we could take things as slow as you want. I'm not taking my words back." Because no matter how much Hunter wanted to know all of Sasha's secrets, they weren't worth making Sasha feel uncomfortable. Hunter wanted to be the person Sasha needed him to be, whoever that was.

Sasha sighed. "No, you need to know. I mean, I'll probably have to tell everyone anyway once we're back, if anything because it might get Nysys out of trouble. The reason I told him I have a power is that I do. I was taken by the Glass Research Company when I was nineteen. They didn't keep me for long because the council was created, and the company disbanded, but it was long enough for them to experiment on me. I thought I left the same as I went in, but I didn't. The problem is that I didn't find out until . . ."

Hunter wanted to pull Sasha into his arms, but he didn't. He wasn't sure how Sasha would take it. "Until?"

Sasha took a deep breath. "I was out hiking with my boyfriend, Cedric. We both loved it, and it was a way to get away from life in the city and our jobs. We were in the forest when we were attacked. I didn't find out until later that it was by a bear shifter. He killed Cedric because Cedric tried to protect me. Then he attacked me, and I . . . blew him into pieces. I'm not sure how I did it, to be honest. I've never done anything like that again. I refused to even try."

"You were afraid." And he probably still felt guilty. He'd managed to save himself, but not his boyfriend.

"Yeah. I don't want to hurt anyone. But it would come in handy if I *could* make this work right now."

Hunter reached out and skimmed Sasha's cheek with a finger. "I know. But we'll get out of here even without you making anyone explode. I promise." And that was one promise Hunter would make sure he kept.

Chapter Six

Sasha didn't want to open his eyes. He wanted to believe he was in his bed instead of in a freaking jungle, already sweating his ass off. He wanted to believe he was going to go to the bar for his shift later rather than having to run for his life.

It didn't work.

He sighed and opened his eyes. Dark rock and green foliage greeted him. He supposed there were worse places to wake up in—like a lab, or next to one of those Beasts guys, probably tied up.

He rolled his head to the side to look at Hunter and froze. Hunter wasn't there.

Sasha sat up and looked around. He had no idea what time it was, but there was enough light outside to illuminate the part of the cave where they'd spent the night. Hunter was nowhere to be seen, though.

Sasha swallowed. Had something happened to him? Was he angry because of what Sasha had said the night before? He hadn't seemed angry, but what did Sasha know? Maybe he didn't like the fact that Sasha hadn't been able to protect Cedric, or that he hadn't tried to learn how to use his power.

Or maybe he was just out there looking for food or making sure the Beasts were still far away.

Sasha snorted when he realized what he was thinking. He'd never been so overly dramatic, not even in his own thoughts. Finding out he was Hunter's mate had messed with his mind—it still was—and he wasn't sure how to deal with it. He needed to pull himself together, though. He and Hunter wouldn't have the opportunity to talk about, well, anything, until they were back home. It would be too distracting, and they needed to leave the cave as soon as possible and cross the Nix shield so someone could pick them up.

Sasha got up and tried not to worry. He didn't want to leave the cave, not even to relieve himself, so he walked as far as he dared into the deeper part of it and did his business there. It still felt like someone was watching him and waiting for the right moment to attack, but at least he wasn't exposed. He doubted Hunter would have left him alone if the Beasts had been anywhere near them, but what did he know? Maybe Hunter hadn't realized and they'd caught him, leaving Sasha all alone in the fucking rainforest to be eaten by a jaguar or whatever wild animal lived around there.

Sasha shook his head. He needed to *stop* thinking about this stuff. He'd be home soon, and he was never going to step foot in a forest again—too many bad memories.

He walked back to the platform and wondered if he should take it down. Probably not. If anything happened, he and Hunter might need to spend another night here, and he didn't want to have to build it again or to sleep on the ground.

The sound of something slithering made him turn around. He did so slowly because he *knew* something was watching him this time. He was sure of it.

He was right.

A huge snake, the biggest he'd ever seen, was entering the cave. It was holding something furry and dead in its mouth, and Sasha briefly wondered if the snake had chosen the cave to have its snack before freaking out.

He pressed his back against the wall and wondered if he should try to get past the snake or run deeper into the cave.

He didn't know where the cave ended, and he didn't want to risk getting lost, but he also didn't want to be the snake's main course. It was big enough that it was a possibility, and he didn't want to risk it.

The snake slithered closer to the platform and dropped the furry thing. Sasha's stomach turned, and he looked away from the blood, but that meant he was staring at the snake now. It was brown, with darker stripes along its mouth and on its entire length. It was kind of beautiful, although Sasha knew he wasn't going to think that when the snake tried to eat him.

The snake stopped moving. Sasha couldn't look away, which was why he noticed it right away when something weird happened. He gaped as the snake started changing, limbs growing out of it while his skin lost it designs.

Then Hunter was standing in front of Sasha, seemingly uncaring that he was buck ass naked. "Good morning. I was hoping to get back before you woke." Hunter turned and leaned down to grab the furry dead thing.

Sasha's gaze went straight to his ass. It was a thing of beauty, and Sasha wasn't sure where to look—the round, pale globes of Hunter's ass, or the dick that was dangling between Hunter's legs.

He licked his lips. All of that could be his. When had he last had sex? He knew it had been with Cedric, so it had been years. He hadn't been able to relax enough to do anything with anyone else, and he'd isolated himself so well that until he'd moved to Gillham, he hadn't even had the opportunity to have any kind of sex. Now that he worked in the bar, he got propositioned at least twice every evening if not more, but he'd never been interested.

He was now. Damn if he was.

Hunter straightened and looked at Sasha. He *had* to have caught Sasha staring, even though Sasha looked away as fast as he could, but he didn't say anything about it. Instead, he held up the furry thing. "I caught this for breakfast."

Sasha stared at it. "Nope."

"What?"

"I'm not eating whatever that is, especially not raw."

"It's a deer. Well, part of it. I didn't want to waste too much time, so I left the rest of the carcass out there. This should be enough for us for breakfast."

"It's raw. And furry." And Sasha was pretty sure he'd puke if he had to eat that. He realized he needed his strength to hike back to the Nix shield, but he'd rather have another protein bar. If there was nothing else to eat, he'd wait until they were back home.

Hunter rolled his eyes. "I'll clean it, of course, and I think we can light a small fire if we do it far enough away from the entrance of the cave. I checked the area before hunting, and there was no one. Come on, Sasha. I'll cook you a nice breakfast. It will be nicer than dinner last night."

Sasha couldn't help but smile. "That wouldn't be hard, since we only ate protein bars."

"Try to be positive, yeah?"

Sasha sighed. "Fine. You can cook that thing. I'm not promising I'll eat it, though. I'll taste it, but that's as far as I'm going for now."

Hunter grinned. "You'll love it."

Sasha watched him move around the cave. He thought Hunter would grab his clothes and put them on, but instead, he stayed naked as he crouched over some of the materials they hadn't needed last night and sifted through them. "You're not going to get dressed?" he asked, hoping his voice was steadier than he felt.

"Not right away. I'm about to get bloody, so I'll clean up outside once I'm done. You can go back to bed if you don't feel like watching my naked ass."

Looking at the ceiling would be safer than having to make sure he wasn't staring, so Sasha clambered onto the platform again and stretched out on his back. He listened to Hunter move around the cave. As Hunter worked, Sasha could smell the scent of burning wood, the sharp scent of blood. Under all that was Hunter's scent, and Sasha wished he were a shifter so he could smell it.

"So, like I said, I checked the area," Hunter said as he worked. "The shield is arranged in a circle, and we're right smack in the middle of it. I'm not sure how wide it is, but I don't doubt the Beasts are still around the shield. They know we have to go back if we want to leave, and they're going to wait for us. It's easier than trying to find us. I think we can manage to sneak by them, though. The shield has to cover a large amount of space because of all the stuff they piled up." Hunter moved closer, and his face appeared above Sasha's. "I'll keep you safe. Don't worry. We'll probably have to make a run for it, but this is my job, and I'm good at it. I'll take you home in one piece."

Sasha smiled without thinking about it. "Thank you."

Hunter's answering smile was soft and said more than his words. "I'd do pretty much anything for you, Sasha. I know you don't trust me, but I'm not lying."

"I trust you." And he wanted to do much more. He couldn't believe he was considering this, but he had a chance at another relationship, at being with someone who didn't care that he had a freak power, or that he was scarred.

But what if something happened to Hunter, too? What if he got hurt while trying to get Sasha out of the jungle, or later, in one of his missions? Could Sasha really go through that again?

Hunter wasn't sure what was going on in Sasha's mind, but

he could see the exact moment Sasha started closing himself off. Was it something he'd said?

He thought back as he went back to work on the deer, but he hadn't said much, just that he wished Sasha would trust him.

Was that it? Did Sasha think he was going to cheat on him? Or was it something deeper and darker? He hadn't been surprised when Sasha had told him about Cedric and what had happened to him. It had been obvious something had traumatized Sasha, and Hunter wasn't sure which one was worse—the time Sasha had spent in that lab or having to watch his boyfriend being killed in front of him without being able to do anything to help him. And even worse, he'd then managed to save *himself*. Hunter knew it hadn't been conscious, but did Sasha see it that way?

Was *that* why he was withdrawing? Was he afraid he'd somehow hurt Hunter or wouldn't be able to help him if he needed it? Or was he afraid to lose Hunter the way he'd lost Cedric?

There was no way for Hunter to know which one it was unless he asked, but he wasn't sure it was the best thing to do. He'd promised he wouldn't push and that he'd let Sasha do things at his own pace, even though it seemed to be a glacial one. But would Sasha ever feel ready at the very least to talk to Hunter? He was content and secure in his isolation. He knew he wouldn't get hurt if he kept to himself because he didn't care for anyone else. Hunter wanted to coax him out, and he wouldn't be able to do that if he didn't push at least a little.

He let it go while he cooked the meat and went outside to wash up. He knew Sasha had been staring at him before, and while he enjoyed the fact that his mate found him stareable, there was no way they could have a serious conversation with him still naked. Besides, if anything happened, he'd rather be wearing his clothes.

He waited until they were sitting on the ground around the fire and eating with their fingers to bring it up again. "It wasn't your fault."

Sasha froze for a second. When he went back to eating, he didn't look at Hunter. "I don't know what you mean."

"Yeah, you do. I can tell you feel guilty about your power kicking in to save you and not Cedric. Did you know you had it?" Hunter already knew the answer to that, but he wanted Sasha to repeat it.

"No," Sasha said, his voice strangled as if it were hard for him to admit that.

"So you had no clue you could save yourself when it happened?"

"No."

"I know you might not want to believe me, but it really wasn't your fault."

"I know."

"Do you?"

Sasha sighed. "Yeah, I do. It took me a while to realize it, but I do. But that doesn't mean I don't *feel* guilty, and I'm not sure how to get over that."

"I wish I could help you."

Sasha finally smiled. "I know. And thank you for that."

Hunter ate another bite of meat. He wanted to know what Sasha thought of them together. Would it be so bad to ask? Sasha could always tell him to fuck off if he didn't want to answer, but Hunter hoped he'd have at least something to give him hope. "Have you thought about us? I mean, us being together? I'm not asking you to bond with me or anything, not right now, but I'd like to know if I at least have a chance. You've been running hot and cold since you arrived, so . . ."

"You have to admit this situation isn't exactly the best one to talk about feelings."

"I know. And you can avoid answering if you want. We can wait to talk about this until we're back home. But this is the first time we've been alone for so long, and I'm afraid you'll go back to your old life once we're back and that it'll be easy for you to ignore me, or to find reasons we shouldn't be together. I'm sure you've already thought about that plenty of times, so why don't we just put everything out here and try dealing with it?"

Sasha cocked his head. "This is really eating at you, isn't it?"

"Of course it is. You're my mate. I want to spend the rest of my life with you, and I'd like to know if you feel the same way, or at the very least, if you'd consider it."

"All right. Let's talk about it." Sasha licked his lips. "I *did* think about it. I don't think I've been able to think about anything else since the picnic. And I *do* want to be with you. I'm scared, though."

Hunter's chest loosened. Sasha wanted to be with him. He could deal with whatever else happened or any obstacle Sasha thought they had—because his mate wanted him. "Of what? If it's of my past and the fact that I had a lot of hookups, I promise you that's over. It's been over since I realized you were my mate. I wouldn't cheat on you even if I wanted to, and I don't. None of those people can compare to you and the way I feel about you. And no, it's not just because you're my mate."

The corner of Sasha's lips curled into a half-smile. "You're so sure that's what I was going to ask?"

"It's a question a lot of humans ask when it comes to being mates. But, Sasha, I've watched you. I know it sounds creepy, but I've been drawn to you even before I got close enough to smell you."

"Because we're mates."

"Because you intrigued me. You're always reserved, but when I see you with Grey, you change completely. You have a beautiful smile, and you're always nice to people."

"Because I could lose my job."

"You're making it hard on purpose."

"You're right, I am. And I'm not worried about your past hookups, or even about the reason you want me." Sasha bit his lower lip and looked down. "I've already lost someone important to me. I'm not sure I could stand going through that again, and the fact that we're in this situation is a good example of what I'm afraid of. What if you go on a mission and you never come back?"

Dammit. That was the one thing Hunter couldn't promise. "I know it's not easy, but trust me, things don't usually go this way. I don't know what happened, why we didn't know the Beasts were sending more men, but we should have, we have eyes and ears everywhere, including in the Beasts. Missions are usually much tamer."

"Usually, but not always."

Hunter dragged his ass toward Sasha and bumped their shoulders together. "Not always. I'm not going to lie to you. This *is* a dangerous job, but I don't want to quit. I like helping people, and I don't want my friends to do this without me."

Sasha leaned his head against Hunter's shoulder and looked up at him. "I get it. I'm just . . . scared."

"I know, and we can talk about it as many times as you need us to. But please, don't use my job against us. I don't want to give up either one." But if he had to, Hunter would choose Sasha. He could always get another job. He'd never get another mate.

Tears were glistening in Sasha's eyes, and Hunter wanted to dry them. He didn't know what else to do or say to help. Sasha's fear was his own, and while Hunter understood it, he couldn't help him get over it or even make it more manageable.

He cupped Sasha's cheeks and rubbed his thumb over his cheekbone. "I'll be as careful as I can. I promise. I want our relationship to work for many, many years. I'm serious about it, more so than I've ever been about anything. I can be a good mate. You just need to give me a chance to show you." He leaned down and gently pressed their lips together.

He'd expected Sasha to move back, but he didn't. Instead, he pressed closer into the contact, and Hunter hoped it wasn't merely physical, that he was finally accepting they could actually work.

He wasn't sure what he'd do otherwise.

Hunter deserved more than what Sasha was giving him right now. Sasha wasn't sure of anything else, but he was sure of that. It didn't matter that his reasons for waiting and keeping the distance between them were good ones or that Hunter was willing to wait. He shouldn't have to.

Hunter was a good man. Sasha didn't care about his past, not even when it came to the other people he'd been with. Everyone had a past, even him. He could easily imagine that Hunter might be jealous of Cedric. Sasha had been in love with him after all, and in a way, he was still carrying a flame.

Or he had been.

Because as much as Sasha had loved Cedric and probably always would, his feelings for him had faded long ago. They were there, but they weren't central to Sasha's life. No one had been in too long. It was terrifying, because opening himself up to love also meant opening up to possible loss and pain, but had Sasha really been living until now? Or had he been hiding from life because it was easier and safer?

He didn't have to think about the answer to that. He already knew it.

He was going to do this. He was going to be with Hunter, and he was going to be happy. "All right."

Hunter blinked. "What?"

"All right. I want to be with you."

Hunter's eyes narrowed, and he stared at Sasha. "Are you sure? I don't want you to do this just because you think you owe it to me."

"I'm not."

"Because I don't care that you're my only mate. If you don't want this, I won't push."

Sasha smiled. "And that's one of the reasons I'm saying yes. I still want to take things slow, and I don't know how I'll react to the first time you'll be sent on a mission, but I still want to try." He looked around. "Although I doubt the next mission can be worse than this one."

"I told you, missions aren't usually this messy. Something happened, and we didn't get the intel we needed. I'm sure Dominic is already looking into it."

"I think I'd be worried even if you were sent to babysit puppies. But I'll try. You were right. I'm not living. It's easier to keep everyone away and avoid hurting, but I can't live the rest of my life like this. I'm only thirty-one. Fifty or something years is a long time to be alone."

"More like a hundred years if we bond."

Sasha grimaced. "That kind of freaks me out, too. But I'm not going to worry about it."

Hunter stroked Sasha's hand. "You know you can always talk to me about anything, right? I meant what I said. I might not have the best track record with relationships since I've never had one that lasted more than a few weeks, but I'm going to do my best. You *deserve* the best, whatever you think. And I don't want you to worry about other people. I won't betray your trust, not when you're giving it to me of all people."

"I never thought you might cheat on me."

"No?"

"No. Even if Grey and Nysys hadn't insisted you wouldn't, I know you're a good guy. You're not the only who's been watching." And while Hunter had sometimes been callous with his hookups, he'd never been mean or cruel. He was a good friend and a good enforcer. He could have left Michael behind easily, even if only to get help, but he hadn't. He'd stuck around, and when they'd been attacked, he'd made sure Michael got home, putting his safety before even Sasha's, who was his mate.

"So . . . we're together?" Hunter asked.

It wasn't like him to be hesitant, but Sasha understood why he was. "Yes. I'm not sure what I'm ready for yet except for leaving this jungle, though."

"We have all the time in the world to figure that out, don't worry. And you're right, leaving the jungle is our first goal right now. There's no way we can think about what we want when we're being hunted." He sighed. "And on that note, we should probably go. The Beasts will no doubt have spent the night shipping out their stuff, so hopefully, there aren't as many of them around this morning."

"Do you think Dominic will send someone today?"

"I don't know. There's no way to find out, not with the communications still down. But if I had to guess, he'll send a Nix to pick us up as soon as they can sense us again, so the sooner we get out of the Nix shield, the better it will be. We could wait here for the enforcers to arrive, but I don't know how long that would take. It's possible it could be days, depending on how much resistance the Beasts offer. No, our best chance to go home soon is to get out of the shield. It's also the most dangerous, though. You have to know that."

Sasha did. He knew the Beasts were sticking around the shield boundary so they could catch them. Damn it. Why hadn't he ever tried to make this fucking power of his work? It could have come in handy right now. He didn't want to lose someone else, not when he might be able to do something about it. He hadn't been able to help Cedric because he hadn't known about his power. This time was different, yet it wasn't.

Hunter kissed Sasha's cheek. "Don't worry too much. I know I said it was dangerous, but this is what I do. I'll protect you."

"I know." And Sasha couldn't wait to go home. He wanted to spend time with Hunter, and not in a jungle all sweaty and dirty. He wasn't sure he was ready to have Hunter in his bed yet, but he definitely wanted more than a few chaste kisses, especially after seeing him in all his naked glory.

Hunter got up and held his hand out to Sasha. Sasha took it, relishing the contact. It was the first time in a while that he'd allowed himself this, and it felt good, especially when Hunter pulled too hard and Sasha tumbled against his chest.

Sasha looked up, and Hunter looked down. After a moment, Hunter wrapped his arms around Sasha and lowered his face, moving slowly, probably to give Sasha the time to move away if he didn't want them to kiss.

But Sasha wanted it.

He pressed closer, and the smile that bloomed on Hunter's face was just a flash before their lips touched. Hunter was gentle, as if he were afraid Sasha might break, and Sasha didn't blame him. *He* felt like he might break. Too many emotions battled in his mind and his chest, and it was almost too much. He felt like he was about to burst open, or possibly cry, and he didn't want that. He didn't want to cry while he was kissing his mate for the first time.

The sound of a rock falling somewhere around the entrance of the cave made both of them jerk apart. A man was coming toward them, a knife in his hand, a wicked grin on his lips. He threw himself on Hunter, who pushed Sasha behind his back.

Sasha reacted on instinct. Images of Hunter wounded or dead ran in his mind, and the next thing he knew, the man with the knife *exploded*.

Pieces of flesh, bones, and things Sasha didn't want to think about dropped to the ground around him and *on* him. He shuddered in disgust and shook himself. The bits that fell off him made a horrible sound as they hit the ground.

Hunter's eyes were wide, and something red and slimy was sliding down his cheek. Sasha swallowed and prayed the meat he'd eaten earlier would stay where it was.

"What was that?" Hunter asked.

"My power."

"How did you do it?"

"I don't know." But Sasha hoped he'd be able to use it again if he needed to. He wasn't going to let anyone hurt Hunter, not if he could avoid it.

Hunter grimaced as he pushed the thing sliding down his cheek off his skin. "Well, that was something."

"I'm sorry."

"What for? You saved me from having to fight that guy."

"Maybe, but it was ... messy." Sasha needed a shower, and he needed it right now. Hunter barked out a laugh. "That's one way to say it. But it's fine. We both already needed a shower anyway. Come on. If this guy found us, the other Beasts are no doubt close by. We need to move."

Hunter was going to have a heart attack. He was going to drop dead if another asshole popped out of the woods and tried to attack him and Sasha. They scared the shit out of him every time, and he kept expecting Sasha to blow them up. It hadn't happened again—yet—but Hunter suspected Sasha's power was fueled by fear. He'd been afraid to die that first time, and he'd blown the bear shifter to pieces. He'd been startled and frightened, and he'd blown the Beast into disgusting bits of gore.

As long as he didn't blow *Hunter* up, it was fine with Hunter.

"Where are they coming from?" Sasha asked as he pushed away from the tree he'd been leaning against. He stepped around the dead man on the ground and came closer to Hunter, taking his hand and checking the knuckles.

"We're close to the shield. They're patrolling it. I'm not surprised. I just wish they'd stay away just long enough that we can pass the damn shield and go home."

"How far away is it?"

"Not much farther." Hunter took Sasha's hand again and pulled him toward the shield. "Come on." He'd memorized the exact spots where the machines that made up the shield were when he'd brought Michael here, so he knew how far they needed to go to finally free himself and Sasha.

He didn't feel anything when they crossed the shield, but he knew they had when Pryderi suddenly appeared in front of them. His arms were stretched out, and the rest of Hunter's team was holding on to him. Hunter could have kissed all of them, but he limited himself to grabbing Pryderi's shirt and looked him in the eyes as he said, "Take me home."

Pryderi did. He shimmered all of them back to the mansion. Hunter let go of him and dragged Sasha into his arms, kissing his forehead and finally relaxing. "Thank fuck. Are you guys going back to the jungle to help with the Beasts?"

Sarah shook her head. "No. We shouldn't even have all

come with Pryderi. We're off this job, and frankly, I'm happy about that. I want to tear all of them apart for what they did to Michael, you, and Sasha."

Hunter frowned. "Michael? What happened? Is he—"

"He's okay. Already healed, and he wanted to come along, too, but he's on bed rest. He's not going anywhere until the doc tells me he can."

"I want to see him."

Sarah wrinkled her nose. "Not until you have a shower. Actually, Pryderi, why don't you shimmer both of them to Hunter's room? That way they won't spread their stink all over the mansion. Unless Sasha would rather go to his guestroom?"

Hunter wouldn't have minded, but he wanted Sasha with him. He wouldn't push if Sasha was more comfortable going to the guest room, though. "Sasha?"

"Your room."

Hunter nodded. He pressed his lips together, because he didn't want to smile like a loon. His team knew Sasha was his mate, but they didn't know what had happened with them while they'd been in the forest. To be honest, Hunter wasn't sure of that, either. He and Sasha had decided they were together and they'd kissed, but they hadn't been able to talk since they'd been interrupted, and Hunter wanted to know where they stood. He realized this wasn't the best moment to talk, though. They both needed showers, food, and sleep, and Hunter was going to have to go find Sarah and Dominic and tell them what happened, as well as write a report.

He hated reports.

Justin moved to hug Hunter, but he stopped before touching him and wrinkled his nose. "God, Sarah's right. You stink." He gingerly patted Hunter's arm. "I'll hug once you don't smell like dead things. And what the fuck is that stuff?"

Hunter looked down. There was a blob of something stuck on his t-shirt. "Uh. I'm pretty sure that's brain." He grinned and took Pryderi's hand. "Ready when you are."

He loved his teammates, but damn if he wasn't glad when he and Sasha were finally alone in his room. He sighed and rolled his head, trying to get the kinks out of the muscles. The platform had been better than sleeping on the ground, but it hadn't exactly been a mattress.

He straightened and looked at Sasha. "Okay, the bathroom's that way. It's not very big, but you'll have plenty of space. Take your time. I can go shower somewhere else." Maybe the gym's shower?

"Or you could shower with me? As long as the stall is big enough."

That, Hunter hadn't expected. "Are you sure?"

"Please. I don't think I'm, well, up for anything, but I don't want this to end yet. I know you probably have a lot of stuff to do and that I need to go home, but I want us to have this moment before things get crazy again."

Thank God. "I don't want you to go yet, so that's good. And I don't expect anything from you. We'll just wash up, and you can borrow some of my clothes. I'll have to go write my report after that, though. You can stay here and sleep if you want, though. I wouldn't mind finding you in my bed once I'm done."

Sasha bit his lower lip. "I think I should go home. I want to check in on Nate and reassure him that I'm okay, see when he's going to need me back at work."

Hunter had expected that. Sasha had his own life, and he needed to go back to it. "I'm not sure when I'll have time to come to you. I mean, I don't want us to be apart, but we don't live in the same town, and even though my team is off this mission, I know we're going to have to check in on the guys who were supposed to tell us what was happening and do damage control."

"I know. It's all right. It's your job, and I have to get used to it, don't I?"

That meant he really wanted to spend time with Hunter in the future, and even though Hunter wanted to push, it was something. It was a step forward. "Come on. I'm ready for that shower. I bet we smell like a herd of sheep."

"And dead bodies," Sasha muttered as he passed by Hunter and walked into the bathroom.

Hunter made sure to give Sasha privacy as they stripped down. They dumped their clothes on the floor, and Hunter didn't look at Sasha. He was going to have to sooner or later, but he wanted Sasha to feel comfortable, and he wasn't sure how to do that. "I'll need to burn these clothes," he said, trying to loosen the tension in the room. Things had been so easy when they'd been in the jungle. They'd had too much to think about to be worried about being embarrassed or not knowing how to behave with each other.

They were safe now, though, and Hunter had no idea where to start.

Sasha went into the shower first. Hunter almost fell because he tried not to look at his ass, and Sasha laughed. "You can look."

"Are you sure? I don't want you to be uncomfortable."

"I'm not. You know I have scars. You've seen the one on my face, and I'm sure you've imagined the ones under my clothes at the very least."

Hunter looked. If the bear shifter who'd attacked Sasha hadn't already been dead, he would have killed him with his own hands.

Like Sasha had said, he'd imagined the scars, but they were worse than he'd thought. Like the one on Sasha's face, they were long and thin, made by claws. They went from

Sasha's neck to his stomach, with one of them ending even lower, on Sasha's groin. It had narrowly missed Sasha's cock.

Hunter swallowed. He didn't say he was sorry. Sasha knew it. He also knew Hunter didn't care about the scars, and Hunter wasn't going to pity him or feel sorry for him. Sasha had gone through hell, and he'd come out the other end alive and in one piece. *That* was what Hunter cared about, what was important.

Hunter slipped under the water and opened his arms. Sasha came without hesitating, wrapping himself around Hunter, plastering their bodies together under the water.

They were where they both belonged, and they'd work out everything else.

Chapter Seven

Sasha rubbed the counter one more time, but he knew it was clean. He just didn't have anything else to do.

He'd swept the floor, had restocked the bottles behind the bar, the fridge, and the freezer. He cleaned all the tables and the counter twice already.

This was the third time.

He sighed and put down the rag. If he kept on polishing the slab of wood, he was going to wear a hole into it.

He'd been behaving like this since Nysys had shimmered him home two days ago. He knew it was ridiculous, but he couldn't help moping around.

He and Hunter had been texting almost non-stop, but it wasn't the same thing. Sasha wanted him close. They hadn't even managed to talk when they'd come back from the jungle. Hunter had showered and had left to talk to Dominic and who knew who else, and Nysys had taken Sasha home. Sasha had wanted to stay, but he understood Hunter needed time to deal with everything that had happened. At least he knew Hunter was safe now. He couldn't feel it because they hadn't bonded yet, but Hunter called and texted every day, and Sasha was making it be enough.

He had to.

He wasn't going to rush Hunter. His job was important to him and to the people who depended on him, and Sasha didn't want to take that away from him, or to take him away from it. No matter how scared he was that he was going to lose him, he needed to get over that and deal with it. Many people were married to cops or enforcers, and they made it work. They learned to live with it. Sasha could do that, too.

And Hunter's absence had given him the time he needed to think and to decide what he wanted. He knew the answer to that now, and he couldn't wait to tell Hunter.

Someone knocked on the door. It was too early for the bar to be open, so Sasha yelled, "We're closed!"

That didn't stop the person at the door from knocking again. Sasha sighed. Some customers just didn't get a hint, or even a yell. "I said we're closed, dammit," he muttered. He knew better than to yell again, though. If this person hadn't understood the first time, they wouldn't go away until Sasha said it to their face.

Just as well. It would give him something to do that wasn't yearning after Hunter and polishing the counter.

He stomped to the door and took a deep breath before opening. He didn't want to scream in the customer's face. That was never good for business.

He swung open the door, his mouth already open, and froze. Hunter was standing in front of him, a bag slung over his shoulder, a smile on his face. His long hair was loose, a sign he wasn't going to work anytime soon, and he looked so good that Sasha wanted to climb him like a tree and never come down. "Hunter?" he stuttered.

Hunter's smile widened. "Hey there."

Sasha resisted the urge to slam the door in his face. "Hey there? That's all you have to say? Why didn't you tell me you were back? Or that you were coming?"

Sasha's hair was tied back because it bugged him while he worked. He wanted to untie it and cover his face with it even though he knew Hunter didn't care about his scar and that he'd already seen it plenty of times when they were in the jungle. It wasn't like Sasha had been careful about that while they were in the jungle. He'd been too worried about staying alive.

Hunter frowned. "I thought you'd be happy to see me."

Sasha threw himself into his mate's arms. Hunter jerked in surprise and caught Sasha just in time. They didn't crash to the ground, but they stumbled.

Sasha didn't care. "Of course I'm happy to see you, dumbass. I just wish you'd told me you were coming," he said against Hunter's neck.

Hunter's arms tightened around him. "You look beautiful, sweetheart. Nothing you can do would make you even more perfect."

Sasha leaned away and rolled his eyes. "You think you're so smooth."

"That's because I am. Can I come in, then? Or are you going to leave me here as if I were just another customer?"

Sasha grabbed Hunter's hand and dragged him into the bar. "*This* is why you should have called me. I would have told Nate I couldn't work tonight. I can't let him down now."

"That's fine." Hunter held his bag out. "See? I have an entire week of vacation with the possibility of extending it if I need more time. If *we* need more time."

An entire week with Hunter. That sounded good, especially since they'd have a bed and electricity this time—and no one would try to kill them. "What are you going to do while I work, then?"

"I already told Grey I'd be in town, so I'll spend some time with him and Patrick. Michael and Pryderi will probably come around, too."

"How's Michael?" Sasha hadn't had the opportunity to talk to him after they'd come back from the jungle, and he didn't have his number. Besides, Michael might be Hunter's best friend, but Sasha didn't know him that well, so he probably wouldn't have called. He'd been worried, though.

"He's fine. He was healed as soon as Nysys got him home, and he's allowed out of bed now. Sarah's still keeping an eye on him, but that's only because she's overprotective. She always said we're like her kids."

"Sarah? She can't be much older than the lot of you."

"Not by much, no. But she loves her job, and it doesn't go well with having kids. I guess she adopted us. Besides, you know how it works with shifters. She looks a lot younger than she is." He looked around. "I've never been in here when it's empty. What time do you open?"

"In a few hours."

"And what are you going to do in the meantime? Is Nate around?"

"No. he had to go out to talk to one of our suppliers. He should be back by the time I need to open, but even if he's not, I can hold the fort for a while without a problem."

Hunter's answering smile was wicked. "So we have at least a few hours to ourselves."

Sasha swallowed. He'd imagined this moment lots of times, but he couldn't believe they were going to do it here, in the bar. There wasn't time to go back home, though, and he needed to stick around just in case. "Breakroom," he croaked. There was a couch there, so at least they wouldn't have to use one of the tables, although the thought was making Sasha horny. He wouldn't be able to focus on his job if he kept remembering what had happened on the table, though, so break room it was.

"In the hallway, right?"

Sasha nodded and let Hunter guide him there. In theory, only the people who worked at the bar could go into the break room, but then, in theory, Sasha shouldn't have sex on the couch there, and it looked like that was exactly what was going to happen.

Hunter didn't need to be told where the break room was.

He opened the door and didn't bother to close it before pushing Sasha onto the couch. Sasha bounced, and Hunter *pounced*.

Sasha laughed as Hunter tried to get rid of his jeans. They couldn't get completely naked just in case someone came by, but Sasha was all for being at least half-naked. It felt good to do this, to laugh and feel light, like the future was bright again instead of the gloomy gray Sasha had thought it would be since he'd lost Cedric. He still loved Cedric, but he had Hunter now, and he was going to allow himself to be happy. It might be cliché, but it was what Cedric would have wanted. He'd loved Sasha as much as Sasha had loved him, and Sasha knew that if their roles had been reversed and he'd been the one to die, he'd have wanted this for Cedric.

"God, I've missed you," Hunter said as he knelt in front of the couch. He'd managed to get Sasha's jeans halfway down his thighs and had given up, but it was enough. He'd exposed Sasha's cock, and after looking up at him for confirmation, he dove on him, wrapping his lips around the head of Sasha's dick and sucking.

Sasha groaned and dug his fingers into Hunter's gorgeous hair.

God, he hoped Nate wouldn't come back sooner than expected.

YOU MAY ALSO ENJOY THE FOLLOWING FROM EXTASY BOOKS INC:

A Demon's Happiness
Catherine Lievens

Excerpt

Esi dumped the dirty bandages into a red plastic bag and grabbed the cleaner. He sprayed a good amount of it on the metal tray and scrubbed it off with paper towels, humming as he worked.

He liked his job. He knew Ilyhas wasn't as enthusiastic about it as he was, and he understood it. He wished he could do something for Ilyhas, but he had no more power here than he'd had when they'd been in Hell. He was just a minion, someone no one noticed.

"Hey, Esi?"

Esi snapped his head up at the sound of a deep voice. He relaxed when he saw it was Cumar. No one noticed him, except Cumar and his friends. That was okay with him. He liked Cumar and his friends, even though he'd been wary in the beginning. He still felt awkward because of the whole sent-to-grab-Cumar thing, but Cumar had waved away his apologies when he'd tried talking to him and had made him promise he wouldn't think about it again. It was surprisingly easy to do, especially with the way Cumar treated Esi as nothing different than his brother's boyfriend and a friend. "Hey. I hope you're not here because you're hurt."

Cumar shook his head. "Nope, I'm good for now."

"Good." Esi looked down. No matter how many times he told himself that Cumar was just a man, like Ilyhas, he was still intimidated. Cumar had been the next in line for the throne. He'd been something of a mystical figure for Esi. He'd heard about him from Ilyhas, who hadn't known much since his brother had left when he'd been a child. It was hard to reconcile the idea he'd made himself of Cumar with the Cumar standing in front of him.

"I was wondering if you were up for lunch," Cumar said.

Esi blinked at him. "Lunch?"

"Yes. You know, that meal you eat about halfway through your day?"

That was new. Cumar had never invited Esi over for anything, not even for a meal. Esi usually ate at the HQ dining hall, like everyone else, sometimes alone, most days with Ilyhas. He knew other people in HQ, but he didn't feel comfortable enough with anyone to eat with them. "I know what lunch is."

"Would you like to eat it with me, then?"

"What about Thailor and Ilyhas?"

"They can join us if they want to, but Thailor was on the phone with Chase when I left him, and that always takes a while. We can grab Ilyhas on the way, though. Actually, it's better if we do that. I need to talk to both of you."

Esi's stomach churned with unease. "Talk to us?"

Cumar slapped Esi's shoulder. "Nothing bad, don't worry. Come on. Do you need me to help you finish cleaning up?"

"No, thank you. I'm almost done."

Esi finished throwing away everything, dumped the gloves he'd been wearing, and washed his hands. He was still uneasy about talking to Cumar. He wanted to know what was happening. Cumar might not think it was bad, but Esi wanted to be the judge of that.

Esi followed Cumar to the dining hall. They snatched Ilyhas along the way, and Esi watched him and Cumar talk. Things were still a bit tense between them, mostly because they didn't know each other anymore. Ilyhas had idolized his brother, but he'd mostly grown up without him, and their relationship had taken a toll. It was good to see them fill the void, though. Ilyhas needed Cumar. He was one of the reasons Ilyhas had decided to leave the palace and move to the human realm, and Ilyhas needed to know it hadn't been for nothing.

They settled at a quiet table in the corner of the hall. Esi could feel people watching them, and he was glad when Cumar offered to bring them some sandwiches rather than have them queue with him. Esi managed to hide behind a fake plant, shielding Ilyhas from most of the stares, and looked at him. "How was your morning?" They worked together in the infirmary, but that didn't mean they saw each other much during the day.

"Okay. Someone came in with an injury from training, but it wasn't bad." Ilyhas smiled. "No blood."

"That's good." Esi knew Ilyhas didn't like the sight of blood. He wished he could do something to get him out of the infirmary, but so far, no other job had popped up in HQ, and he was terrified about the thought of Ilyhas working somewhere else. He needed the protection Cumar and Jadon were giving him. Some of the warriors weren't happy having him there, but they stayed away because they knew what would happen if they didn't. The demons outside the HQ wouldn't be that nice, though, and Esi didn't want Ilyhas to get hurt.

"What about you?"

Esi shrugged. "Mostly visits with wounded warriors. I changed some bandages, things like that."

Ilyhas grimaced. "I'm sorry."

"Don't be. I like the job."

"How can you? There's blood, and people who don't want you to touch them just because of who you are."

Esi's heart broke a little. "That only happens with you, love."

Ilyhas grimaced. "That's what I suspected." He sighed. "I don't know what else I can do to make them see I'm not my father. I mean, I barely knew the man. It's not like he had even an ounce of paternal instinct or even that he wanted to be a father."

Esi patted Ilyhas' hand. "I know."

Ilyhas flopped back in his chair. Esi opened his mouth to say more, but Cumar arrived, holding a tray and napkins stuffed in his mouth. He put the tray down, and Esi barely managed to grab the bottle of water that rolled off it. Cumar got the napkins out of his mouth and put them down. "Thanks. I hope neither of you thinks I have cooties."

"What did you want to talk about?" Esi asked once they were settled down to eat.

Cumar rolled his eyes and stuffed his sandwich into his mouth. Ilyhas arched a brow. "Cumar wanted to talk?" he asked.

Cumar swallowed. "Yeah. Thailor and I are being sent on a mission. It's not in the city, and I don't know how long we'll be gone."

Ilyhas put his sandwich down. He looked a little green, and Esi knew it was because he didn't like the thought of Cumar being away, both because it would leave him without his biggest protector and because Cumar could be hurt, or worse. "What?" he croaked.

Cumar put his sandwich down and squeezed Ilyhas' shoulder. "It'll be fine. You know Thailor and I are good at our job, and I'm not leaving you on your own. You have Esi, and you have Chase and Yo'ash's numbers. I also talked to Jadon, and he agreed to keep an eye on things and you. I'll give you his number so you can call him if you need it. And

I want you to call him, Ilyhas. No trying to solve whatever happens on your own, okay?"

Ilyhas cleared his throat. "I'm not a child."

"I know. I also know you don't tell people you're hurting or that you have a problem. Well, except for Esi, but he keeps your secrets, so it's not useful. I need you to be safe, though. I won't be able to focus on my job if I don't know that you are. Please. Promise me you'll go to Jadon if anything happens."

Ilyhas nodded. Esi would have promised it himself if Ilyhas hadn't. He might not like the thought of having to rely on other people, but he knew he and Ilyhas wouldn't have any idea how to deal with the world in this realm. They still relied on Cumar, Yo'ash, and their friends to make it, and even though they were trying hard, that wouldn't change for a while.

Cumar smiled. "Good." He dropped his hand and grabbed his sandwich again. "I know life hasn't been easy for you since you got here. I remember how it was in the beginning. But you have me, and you also have friends."

Ilyhas snorted. He was playing with a bit of lettuce that had fallen from his sandwich, and Esi knew he wasn't going to finish eating it. He stopped eating when he was stressed.

"It's true," Cumar insisted.

"You have friends, Cumar. I don't. I only have you and Esi, and neither of you are actually friends."

"You don't see it, but Chase, Yo'ash, Thailor, Aiden and Caelan are your friends. I know you've been keeping them at a distance, but that doesn't mean they don't like you. They respect the fact that you need some time to get used to this realm, but they're there if you need them. As is Jadon."

"How did you manage that? I can't imagine he's looking forward to babysitting us."

Cumar grinned. "I might have told him I wouldn't accept the job if I weren't sure the two of you would be safe."

"And he gave in."

"He knows I'm the best, and he needs me there. Really, Ilyhas. There's nothing to worry about."

Esi hoped that was true.

About the Author

Catherine lives in Italy, country of good food and hot men. She used to write fantasy as a child, but it was reading her first gay erotic romance novel that made her realize that that was what she really wanted to write.

After graduating from college in English language and translation, she divides her day between writing, reading, taking care of her son and reading some more.

You can find her on Facebook and Twitter or on her website: authorcatherinelievens.wordpress.com

Email: lievens.catherine@gmail.com

Newsletter: http://eepurl.com/c-uvKn

Printed in Great Britain
by Amazon